EACH AND EVERY SPARK

CLAIRE SWINARSKI

Quill Tree Books
An Imprint of HarperCollinsPublishers

HarperCollins Children's Books, a division of HarperCollins Publishers,
195 Broadway, New York, NY 10007

HarperCollins Publishers, Macken House, 39/40 Mayor Street Upper,
Dublin 1, D01 C9W8, Ireland

Quill Tree Books is an imprint of HarperCollins Publishers.

Each and Every Spark
Copyright © 2026 by Claire Swinarski
All rights reserved. Manufactured in Harrisonburg,
VA, United States of America.
No part of this book may be used or reproduced in any manner whatsoever without written permission except in the case of brief quotations embodied in critical articles and reviews. Without limiting the exclusive rights of any author, contributor, or the publisher of this publication, any unauthorized use of this publication to train generative artificial intelligence (AI) technologies is expressly prohibited. HarperCollins also exercises their rights under Article 4(3) of the Digital Single Market Directive 2019/790 and expressly reserves this publication from the text and data mining exception.
harpercollins.com
ISBN 978-0-06-332178-6
Typography by Andrea Vandergrift
25 26 27 28 29 LBC 5 4 3 2 1
First Edition

For my two favorite historians:
Benjamin Swinarski, who loves history
more than any other kid I know,
and Mark Courchane, who always knew I could do it.

Beauty will save the world.
—FYODOR DOSTOEVSKY

September, present day

"PENNY!"

Penny Marks squeezed her eyes shut as tightly as she could. Maybe if she lay still in her creaky bed, nobody would know she was there. Maybe *she* could forget she was there.

"Penny!"

She tried to remember what her seventh-grade gym teacher had said last year when they talked about post-exercise meditating. Something about stillness being the key. Or was that Father Ariel talking about prayer in confirmation class? Either way: stillness. She focused on the brash, rattly Paris traffic outside the apartment window. She'd always thought of Paris as jazz music and crumbling croissants and the gentle flow of the Seine, but that was before she'd been forced to move there. It was really all taxi horns and chatty tourists. Paris, like so many other things, was more jarring up close.

"Penny Lane! Bus is *leaving*!" her dad hollered.

Okay, even *she* couldn't stay still at that. She had to roll her eyes. It wasn't like they were seriously going to leave without her.

"Come on," she heard her oldest brother, Matthew, say. "Let's go."

"I'm hungry," her other brother, Mason, insisted.

Penny listened to the typical clatter of her dad and two brothers getting shoes, sweatshirts, wallets, keys. She heard Matthew drop his phone and swear, and her mom snap at him for swearing.

"Last call, Penny Lane!" her dad called chipperly.

Still. Still as a stone. Maybe the earth could open a giant hole and let her sink into it. Sending her in some kind of time-zone warp back to America, where she belonged. Or maybe her mom would burst in and announce that this cross-planet move had been a giant mistake, renounce her fancy art museum job, and they could all get on the first plane back to Wisconsin. First class, this time. Penny's knees still hadn't recovered from the eight-and-a-half-hour flight two days ago.

"I'm staying here!" she finally yelled back, letting her eyes crack open slightly. "It's a protest." When they'd landed, they couldn't get a train from the airport due to a strike. Dad had called France the land of protests. Look at her—fitting right in.

"Fine," Dad responded. "Just don't go on a hunger strike. We haven't even had a croissant yet! Au revoir!"

More clitter, clatter, cluster, and the shutting of a door. Only the quiet *tap-tap-tap* of her mother typing on her laptop.

She closed her eyes again and pictured her old room in her old house. Her paintings on the wall. Her lavender bedspread. Someone *else* lived in their house now. Maybe the renters had already rearranged things in Mom's old art studio, covering up where Penny had done bright pink handprints to the left of the window. And Erin had already squeezed her way into being Rosalie's new best friend. Penny was sure of it. They were probably at the pool right now, floating on their backs and planning out how to conquer eighth grade.

She waited for her dad to pop his head back in and call for her again, but the apartment stayed quiet. She sat up.

Padding out into the kitchen, she saw her mom at the scratched-up kitchen table. Mom's laptop was open in front of her and she typed furiously, her bright blue nails flying across the keys.

"Did they seriously go?" Penny asked. The apartment

felt gigantic without her two gangly brothers sprawled out over the sofa arguing about soccer statistics.

Mom laughed. "Kid, are you joking? Dad called for you a thousand times! I thought you were protesting."

"They actually *left*?" Go figure. They were probably all having a blast, taking photos to send home to their friends and exploring the new neighborhood. She couldn't even say the word *arrondissement*. Honestly, she couldn't really say *anything* in French, which added to her list of Reasons Why Moving to France Was a Bad Idea. She tried her hardest, but her throat just didn't make those guttural French sounds.

"You snooze, you lose," Mom muttered, returning to her typing. "I told them to bring us home dinner."

"What am I supposed to do?" she whined.

"Penny, they *asked* if you wanted to go. I need to get some work done. Want to see this painting I'm teaching about next week?"

She did, actually. In her loud, boisterous family, Penny had always connected most with her mom. They both loved art, they both brought books to the boys' soccer games, and they both thought *Great British Baking Show* was the best series on Netflix.

But Mom was now Enemy Number One. Who woke up one day, surrounded by her three kids who still needed her, and decided it was the perfect time to accept a fellowship teaching art history while researching on the side at the Institut National d'Histoire de l'Art for a year?

"No," said Penny shortly.

Mom finally stopped typing and looked up at her. Penny just stared back, hoping her bad attitude was showing. She could do a great annoyed face when she had to.

"All right," Mom said after a long pause. "Maybe I can take a break. Frown off. Shoes on. Let's find a pastry."

When Mom and Dad first sat Penny and her brothers down to tell them about the Paris plan, Penny had thought they were talking about a *vacation*. She'd pictured wandering the Louvre with her mom, pointing out the Rembrandts that people usually missed in their dash for the Mona Lisa. Madeline had come to mind, and Miss Clavel: "In an old house in Paris that was covered in vines, lived twelve little girls in two straight lines." She'd never been to Europe; Dad traveled sometimes for work, but their family didn't go much of anywhere besides the Wisconsin Northwoods every Fourth of July.

Then when Dad said it was to teach for a *year*, Penny almost started crying. Mom was going to be gone for a whole year? Who would bake brownies with her on Tuesday nights to distract her from the fact that she no longer had painting lessons since she'd quit? Who would listen to the ins and outs of the endless drama between Erin and Rosalie, who were friends one day and enemies the next? Who would be on her side when her brothers were ganging up on her? Who would take her shopping for her eighth-grade graduation dress, and who would take her to the Art Institute of Chicago for her birthday? Who would go grocery shopping and make dinner—*Dad*? They'd have to survive off Culver's. Dad was great and all, but his idea of cooking was preheating the oven for a frozen pizza. He did his own jobs, like mowing the lawn and coaching the soccer teams and getting spoons out of the garbage disposal if they fell in. He had his things. But he was no *Mom*. And that wasn't even to mention school—the class parties Mom always volunteered for; the PTO fundraisers she ran. The Marks family would fall right off its axis without Mom for an entire year. They'd have a clean garbage disposal, but nothing to *eat*.

Then, as Dad started talking about how this would be a huge adjustment but they'd all make special family memories in Paris—about how, yes, they had a lot to learn about the language but they would all start doing some app together in the mornings to prepare, about how he knew Penny would love seeing the ballerinas that Degas had painted in person—she put it together.

They were *all* going.

Mom would miss all of those things, and so too would Penny. They were renting an apartment and living in Paris for in an entire year. They were renting out the house. They'd all be homeschooled online, with Mom and Dad filling in the curriculum cracks.

Last year at Fernridge Falls Middle had been brutal, and Penny knew that was part of why Mom and Dad wanted to whisk them across the ocean. There'd been a lot of hushed voices and biting comments, school board meetings that made it into the news, and articles being written about why Fernridge Falls, Wisconsin was, in one guy with big ears and a nasally voice's opinion, "the perfect representation of issues facing America's school system." Parents wanting books off shelves, and librarians getting mad, and then—the thing with the art program. "Jocelyn James," her mom muttered, as if she was saying "Darth Vader" or something. Jocelyn James at school board meetings, Jocelyn James with her sharp red nails, Jocelyn James on every school board campaign sign in town. She promised if she won, they'd ax art classes, because they didn't *prepare kids for the future*. They needed to focus on *core classes*, she kept saying, that would help kids get *real jobs*. She promised all kinds of things that made Mom fidget and Dad reach over and squeeze her shoulder when they saw Jocelyn on the local news.

Penny had heard her parents talking about the possibility of taking her out of Fernridge Falls public schools. But man, she thought they meant *St. Mary*'s. Or Trinity, where they wore uniforms. Not another *country*.

And then Mason had gotten sick. Really sick. A kind of sick Penny didn't like to think about, with an ambulance and medicine bottles and a hospital room you weren't allowed to enter until you scrubbed your hands to a nurse's standards. He was fine, now. "Doing-really-great," Mom would say perkily, whenever someone asked how he was. Like it was all one word. But she knew it had added to the stress of the year, way more than Jocelyn James had.

In other words: Mom and Dad were fresh-start shopping.

Penny could usually depend on her brothers to be self-centered enough to throw a fit. But they just *grinned*, congratulating their mom.

"What about soccer?" Penny said to Mason accusingly. He had been hoping to make varsity next year as a measly freshman, even though he'd missed a lot of the season last year and had to wear a hearing aid now. But still—his chances were actually halfway decent; the Marks boys were a soccer dynasty. Dad had coached their select teams for years before they got to high school.

"They have soccer in Paris," he said. "They call it football."

"Everyone knows that," she snapped. "Matthew? It's your last year in high school! You want to miss prom? Graduation? *Courtney?*" Matthew had a glamorous girlfriend, who had just gotten her driver's license and drove around the neighborhood in her dad's bright red BMW. She usually looked at Penny like she was something she'd stepped in by accident.

"Paris is the most romantic city in the world! Maybe she can visit. Can we take a weekend trip to Normandy?" he asked excitedly. "To see where the Allies landed during World War II?"

"Of course we can!" said Mom. "It's easy to get to a lot of places from Paris. The European train system is amazing, we'll just—"

Penny got up from the table, walked to her room, and shut the door. As usual, her family barely even noticed she'd left. She sat on her bed, hugged her pillow, and listened to them going on without her on the other side of the door. They were probably happy she'd disappeared; now they could be excited without Annoying Penny dragging them down.

She stayed in her room the rest of the day, trying to read the Hunger Games prequel but mostly just googling *downsides of homeschooling* and *Paris murder rates*. She made sure to text her mom the grisliest news stories she could find.

That night, as Penny lay awake in her bed, her door opened softly. She slammed her eyes shut, pretending to be asleep, but Mom came in anyway and sat on the edge of her bed.

"Penny," Mom whispered. "You awake?"

Penny kept her breathing as slow and even as she could.

Mom reached over and put her hand on her head, brushing back her hair just slightly. Penny wanted to lean in to her soft, cool palm, but she hesitated.

"It will be an adventure, kid," Mom said quietly. "The adventure of a lifetime. And we'll be in it together. All right?"

Penny stayed still until Mom slowly got up and left the room. Nobody asked her if she wanted an adventure. Nobody asked her anything at all.

"Just the right amount of crumble," Mom said in her best Paul Hollywood voice. The café they sat in had a giant case of every pastry imaginable, so she and Mom had picked a few to split. Mom was currently taste-testing the mille-feuille, a layered dessert of puff pastry and vanilla cream. She and Penny always pretended to be *Great British Baking Show* hosts when they tried new desserts.

"The texture's terrible," said Penny, putting on her Prue voice.

"Prue would never call something terrible. She's too nice."

"She would if she'd been kidnapped."

"You know, Penny," her mom said, a slight smile in her eyes, "most kids would be *excited* about a trip to Paris. Especially ones that liked art." A waiter pushed past their small table quickly, balancing an entire tray of filled-to-the-brim cappuccinos on his shoulder.

"You know, Mom," she responded flatly, "most kids aren't kidnapped against their will and forced to live in foreign countries."

"For the last time, parents can't kidnap you."

"They can too! They're the most common suspects!"

"Have you been watching those weird true crime YouTubes again?"

"Mom."

"My *point*," Mom said, "is that you could try and see the bright side of things."

Penny knew what that meant. It was parent-ese for "I'm sick of your whining. Please be happy so that I can go back to my own fantastic life." But if it was Penny's job to remind her mom what a horrible idea this was, she'd be happy to comply.

"I know this is hard," Mom said softly. "Moving—and it wasn't just moving, was it? It's moving to an entirely new place. New language, new culture, new time zone . . . it's a lot."

Penny just shrugged.

"I think if you give it a try, you might be able to find something good about living in Paris," Mom said. "If nothing else, then these desserts, right? And the art museums? Pastries and art are two of your favorite things."

Penny looked at Mom. In all fairness, it was hard to be mad at her mom, who'd basically been the greatest mom in the universe until she accepted this job a couple of months ago. Even when Mason was at his sickest and taking up a lot of her time, she'd *always* been there for Penny. She'd been at every art show, driven her to every painting class, and never said no to having Rosalie sleep over. When her brothers made fun of her for her never-ending pile of library books, Mom always had her back. And when Jocelyn James had finally won and the thing had happened with Mrs.

Marley—well. She didn't even like to think about that. But Mom had let her sleep in her bed with her, kicking Dad to the couch, and they'd stayed up half the night watching *Beat Bobby Flay* and drinking milkshakes, not letting any of the boys in.

But still. They couldn't even *find* an art teacher here who would teach in English. Not couldn't, but *wouldn't*. The French, Penny was learning, could be a bit snobby about their language.

And besides, Penny was starting to think she might be done with painting. As in, not just "taking a break," like Mom had told Mrs. Marley after that horrible day Penny didn't like to think about. As in, done for good.

She hadn't said it yet to Mom, who was still on the hunt for a painting teacher for her. She hadn't mentioned it to Rosalie either, who had come over to help her pack and asked why she wasn't bringing her brushes. But her little "break" that she'd insisted upon was starting to feel not so little.

"Come on," Mom said, sighing at Penny's stony silence. "Let's get back. I have more work to do." She left some euros on the table, linked arms with Penny, and guided her down the windy Parisian street. They'd gone pretty far from the apartment they were renting and had to wander back toward the second arrondissement, past more bakeries but also ramen shops, bubble tea stands, and Italian restaurants. Paris was French to its core, but it was so many other things too—almost like a mixed salad of cultures and languages and ideas. Things didn't blend together, they stood out vibrantly, each making whatever it was next to seem funkier. There was even a giant Nike store, the signature swoop glaring out over the street.

"Oh, wow," Mom said, nodding at a large gray building. "Lycée Victor Hugo. He wrote *Les Misérables*! You love that musical! This school is named after him. Maybe he went here, or helped pay for it?"

Penny kept her face guarded. Okay, fine—she *did* love the musical that book inspired. Eponine singing "On My Own" . . . how could she not? It was probably the most played song on her iPhone. But she wasn't giving her mom the satisfaction of reacting.

Mom paused to read an off-white plaque hanging on the wall while Penny let her eyes wander. Her mother had picked up French way quicker than she had, since she had to use it at work so much.

"It's acknowledging that kids from here were taken by the Nazis," Mom said. "Wow. *Students*, who went here. They were deported with the help of the French government."

"Deported where?"

"To death camps. Mostly Auschwitz, I think—in German-occupied Poland."

Okay, *that* sent a shiver down Penny's spine. She knew her history. Well, kind of. She'd had to read a book about the Holocaust in school last year. Her teacher hurried over some of the details because Lila Porter looked like she was going to throw up from the photographs. But was that in France too? She couldn't remember.

"The French did that? Got rid of their *own* kids, just because they were Jewish?" asked Penny.

"Yes, they did. Paris was occupied by the Germans in the early 1940s. They arrived in . . . 1939? 1940? Oh, Matthew would yell at me." Penny's seventeen-year-old brother was a total nerd. *World War II in Color* was his favorite show. He wanted to major in history at college next year.

"I *know* that. But the French *helped*?"

"Well . . . kind of. It's complicated, kid. There were good guys and bad guys, like every other country, at every other time. But there were a lot of bad guys, and the things they did were . . . terrible. Wow. You think Paris, you think pastries, right? You forget about this. The *history*."

They stood and stared at the sign for just a moment

longer. Mom was right. Paris wasn't just pretty; all sunsets and crepes, perfectly tied scarves and the Eiffel Tower in the background. It had a history, one much longer than anything Penny had ever really thought about. Something awful had happened, right here, where she stood. She could almost feel it in the air—a thick scent of terror, hiding behind the cold walls of the school in front of her.

"Come on," said Mom, after taking a quick photo to show Matthew. "Let's get back. Your dad will be home soon, and wondering where we ran off to."

That night, as Penny tried to get ready for bed, she found herself staring out the window to the back alley behind the apartment. Who knew what had happened there? Right there, on this street, in 1940? Kids like her, being rounded up? It gave her the shivers. She pressed her hand to the screen, letting the cool air of the October night seep through her fingers.

November 1943

MARIE BONNET PRESSED her hand to the window of her small apartment. There was a centimeter of ice across it, thick and sparkling. The flowers that she had brought home from the market last week were frozen in their jar. It had been a silly thing, to spend what little precious money her sister Héloïse gave her, meant for eggs and milk, on flowers. But Maman had always thought spaces should be made lovely.

The window looked out on their street, a street that had once been so cheerful. Rue de Vivienne had been lined with florists, shops, and friends waving to one another. Every morning, Henri the baker had dragged out his cart, selling croissants and baguettes to passersby. He would pretend to pull a franc from behind Marie's ear, before francs were so scarce and bread was nowhere to be found without a ration card. His cat would hide under his cart. It was all so long ago. A cart full of croissants—Marie couldn't even imagine such a thing, these days. She couldn't even remember what Henri's voice sounded like.

Now, all Marie saw was gray. Gray cobblestones, gray buildings, gray boots of German soldiers, chatting in that aggressive language she hated so much. German sounded like someone trying to get something out of their throat. Rue de Vivienne was as gray as a storm cloud, and the only pop of color in Paris came from the bright red Nazi flag that hung over the Ritz hotel.

Even the sky was gray—not much else could be expected from a Parisian November. Autumn felt especially quick and cold this year, though, with so little coal to go around. Marie went to bed with a chill and woke the same way. The cold seeped into her bones, making her teeth chatter so hard she worried they'd snap out of her mouth.

"I'll try to get more coal," Héloise, said through her own clattering teeth, pulling her sweater tight around her. "But . . ."

But it was hard. *Everything* was hard to get in Paris. Things that Marie had once had without thinking. A fire in the hearth every day; *of course*. A warm croissant for breakfast; *of course*. Papa coming home from a long day of work ready to swing her onto his lap; *of course*. The war had stolen all of her *of course*s.

"You'll be late?" she asked. Héloise's hours had become longer and longer; every penny was needed to be put toward food. Héloise worked at the Ritz, the most glamorous hotel in all of Paris. In all the world, if Héloise was to be believed. But cleaning the toilets of les Boches didn't sound very glamorous to Marie.

The Nazi soldiers had begun staying at the hotel almost as soon as they'd arrived. They'd taken over the beautiful suites, trampling the carpet with their boots and ordering the maids around. Marie hated that her sister had to make their beds and dust their mantels. She knew Héloise hated it too. But they hated the sounds of their rumbling stomachs more.

Her sister pointed at her. "Go to school. I won't have all of Paris thinking I'm raising a street girl."

Marie rolled her eyes. She loved to learn; she really did. But school had only gotten more and more dull. Especially for girls. Nobody noticed if she wasn't there. So many had left, anyway; off to be with cousins in the country, or off to wherever the Germans took people. The classrooms were becoming emptier and emptier; fewer and fewer voices were singing praises to the marshal and learning how to be good little French housewives. It bored Marie to tears.

"I mean it, Marie," said Héloise. "School. Au revoir."

"Au revoir," Marie murmured, pressing her hand once more to the window as the door clicked shut.

It was only a minute or so later that the door slammed back open.

"Oh, Marie," said Héloise. "I'm the worst, the absolute worst in the world. I—well, I didn't *forget*...."

Marie hid a smile. "Of course you did."

"I didn't! I'm sorry." Héloise raced over to her, leaned down, and planted a hard kiss on her cheek. "Happy birthday, my sister."

Birthday. As if silly things like thirteenth birthdays mattered anymore. The last birthday Marie had enjoyed . . . she couldn't even remember it. Her ninth, she supposed; but even then, things felt thick and strange—like just before a terrible thunderstorm, when everyone is hiding under awnings and glancing at the clouds before they erupt. There was something floating in the air, then, almost as if a fog had been gently placed upon all of Paris. People were worried; they'd walk down the streets with tighter smiles and quicker paces, the calls of floral vendors seemed stilted, and the very sun didn't seem to shine as bright.

It had been the last birthday before the Germans had come.

To remember a birthday with Maman, Marie had

to think much further back. Maman had gotten that cough that turned into sickness that turned into death when Marie was only six. In truth, there were days she had a hard time even picturing her mother. She had to look at the one photograph they had—Maman and Papa's wedding photo, the old black-and-white picture that was fraying at the edges. Maman wasn't smiling, which certainly wasn't how Marie remembered her.

But Marie's thirteenth birthday would be similar to her twelfth. Perhaps their friend Adrien could snatch a bit of leftover brioche from Café Fleur-de-Lis, where he served coffee. Maybe Héloise would read aloud to her from *The Story of Jeanne d'Arc*, her favorite book. Marie knew she was far too old to be read to; after all, she could read perfectly well herself. But there was something so soothing about Héloise reading it to her, her sister's calm, confident voice blocking out even the loudest of German boots on the streets below. Especially when she was telling the tale of Jeanne d'Arc, the bravest hero France had ever had.

When Marie was younger, before Maman had died, they'd visit her favorite painting of the saint in the Louvre. Marie loved to stare at Jeanne's defiant eyes and the flag in her hands. Jeanne wasn't quiet and dainty; she was bold and courageous, unafraid to fight for her country. Her tattered copy of Jeanne's story was Marie's most precious possession. She'd brought it into her bedroom the day after Papa left and kept it under the bed she shared with Héloise, taking it out nearly every night to flip through the pages and try to let some of Jeanne's courage seep into her bones.

"I'm sorry," Héloise said. "Oh, Marie, I was almost to the bottom of the stairs when I saw the newspaper with the date. Forgive me. I'll bring you home something sweet from the hotel, if I possibly can."

Marie shook her head. "Don't get into trouble."

Her sister bit her lip. "I said *if* I can. I didn't promise. Now, have a good day—at *school*."

Marie had never really liked school. Long before the Nazis came. She much preferred to learn from the books Papa read to her at home.

Papa was—had been—*was* a storyteller; he wrote books for children about animals that dwelled in the countryside of Provence. His most famous, *Le Petit Lapin Rose*, was the only reason Marie and Héloise had the apartment they did. *The Little Pink Rabbit* was the story of a baby bunny that was too afraid to leave its burrow. Instead of living in the dangerous woods, he makes his hutch lovely, bringing in flowers and decorating his walls with beautiful paintings. Papa had dedicated it to Marie's maman, who always made the world, he said, a little more beautiful. Mamans and papas all over Paris read it to their little ones as they tucked them in for the night, willing them to stay as safe and sound as *le petit lapin rose*.

But Papa was gone; he had been sent off to Germany to work at the beginning of the year. "What kind of work could a writer for children possibly do in Germany?" he had asked but hadn't been answered with anything except an order to pack a few things and get on the train. "They don't have a mother," he'd told the German soldier, trying his best to speak that hideous language. He'd gestured toward the girls. "Nein mutter. Nein mutter!" But it hadn't made a difference. The Bonnet girls hadn't received word since—not even a letter. There was no one to call, nobody they could pester. The train had come, and he was gone, with thousands of other fathers and brothers and uncles. Off to the land of *les Boches*, of hand signals and *Heil Hitler*.

Héloise had promised him that she would care for Marie, and she had. Héloise was lucky for the job at the Ritz, which always had food and coal for heat. It was the Ritz, after all. Where princes came to stay when they visited Paris. Where Coco Chanel herself lived, although she spent too much time with the Germans, in Héloise's whispered opinion.

But Marie hadn't promised she'd keep going to school. And as much as she'd disliked it before, she loathed it all the more now. Her teacher, Monsieur Bassot, led "Maréchal, Nous Voilà!" with such gusto it made Marie want to spit at him. She hated that they had to praise the great marshal, the one who had left Paris to the Germans and taken off for Vichy. He'd gone from a big war hero in the past to now being a traitor.

That was where most of the French government had fled, according to Héloise; they were pampering themselves at a glamorous retreat while ordinary Parisians waited in line for food. If it weren't for the marshal, France could actually have fought back, and maybe it wouldn't be overrun with *les Boches*. Maybe there would be a cake for her birthday instead of scraps, and maybe she wouldn't have to wear her thickest wool layers indoors. Maybe Papa would be home.

Nobody wanted to talk about the missing. Not about Madame Stein, who had taught Marie her math lessons last year. Not about Papa, either, and not about her friend Sarah, who always let Marie glance over her shoulder during particularly hard exams. Not about Henri the baker. Nobody wanted to talk about the flower boxes that lined the rue, the flowers inside wilting and dead from lack of care. Nobody wanted to talk about the fact that they were so cold they could hardly think over the chattering of their teeth, even though it was only November. Nobody wanted to talk about the loud *clunk, clunk, clunk* of boots as they marched past the school doors, or about how the holidays this year were sure to be the same sad, sorry affair they'd been last year. Nobody, in Marie's opinion, wanted to talk about anything important at all. Even Papa, before he left, had reminded them to keep quiet, keep still, keep their heads down. "It will be over by Christmas," he had muttered that June when the soldiers first arrived. Well, here they were, nearly three Christmases later.

If Maman were here—

No. Marie shut her eyes tightly. She didn't like to think about things like that.

Marie had been so young when Maman died that the memories of her had started to slip through her fingers. She remembered the way Maman smelled, like the rosewater perfume she insisted on wearing every single day, and the way she'd shut her eyes and smile when she took a bite of a croissant dipped in honey. She remembered the way Maman's fingers would fly across her rosary beads as she prayed for protection over her household. She remembered the way she'd turn on the radio and dance to Charles Trenet, her dress flying around her legs, picking up Héloise and Marie in her arms and spinning until they shrieked with dizziness. She remembered Maman taking them to the Louvre—not just to see the *Mona Lisa* and the *Venus de Milo*, but the lesser-known paintings that she loved so much. She'd always remind them to *linger* over paintings. To step back and breathe them in, admire the light, and let them say something to you.

But the cough had come quick, and with it, the long afternoons on the canapé and the doctor shaking his head. And then the Mass at Notre-Dame-de-Bonne-Nouvelle, long and solemn. Maman would have wanted more singing. That much, Marie was sure of.

Maybe she remembered more than she thought.

And she knew this too, the way she knew the sun would rise in the morning: Maman would not have sung praises to the marshal.

The moment school was out, Marie burst from the doors and hurried toward the Café Fleur-de-lis. Her own sister may have forgotten her birthday, but she knew who wouldn't.

She made sure to carefully step to the side of the sidewalk as German soldiers clicked past her. Les Boches wanted Parisians to move out of the way, giving them rule of the walk. Just last week Josette from school hadn't been paying attention, and a German had kicked her so hard that she fell into the gutter.

When she got to the café, Marie pressed her face to the glass, her breath creating a slight circle of fog. Inside were Germans, Germans, more Germans—sipping the fake coffee made of acorns that Héloïse proclaimed to be disgusting. Marie wouldn't know; she thought all coffee was disgusting. There were a few other men sitting and writing, huddled around the potbelly stove that gave the café its warmth. Adrien had told her that the owner knew how to get black market coal, and that he'd try to get some for her and her sister.

Marie and Héloïse had known Adrien Vannier since they were born; he was only a year older than Héloïse. He'd grown up in the bright blue apartment next door, the one with the crumbling window boxes and beautiful brass door knocker. He lived there still. His father had died when he was a baby, and Maman and Papa would always check in on his mother—making sure she had enough bread, enough coal, enough chatter over cups of coffee. Adrien was obnoxious and silly; like any other boy in the neighborhood.

He'd tugged on Marie's braids as she passed by, and teased Héloise about constantly having her nose in a book. But since their mothers had died, one right after the other, he'd become less of a tease and more of a big brother. When the Nazis had come marching down the Champs-Élysées, he'd stood there with the girls, silently squeezing their hands. Now that Papa was gone, he'd been checking in on them constantly. His was the most comforting face in all of Paris.

Now Adrien worked as a waiter at the café. He was the closest thing to a brother Marie had ever had. And who wouldn't want a big brother?

She knocked on the window and he glanced over, a half smile tugging on his lips. One of the soldiers snapped at him in ruddy French, the guttural German accent wrapped around his words like a rope. Adrien nodded, hurried over with his bill, and dipped outside for just a moment.

"The birthday girl," he said.

Marie grinned. "All I want for my birthday is for you to spit in the coffee of just one German."

Last year, Adrien would have laughed. Now his brow furrowed, and he hushed her.

"You could get thrown in jail for saying such a thing," he said. "You think because you're a child, they'd let it pass? Think again." The Germans did seem particularly angry lately. More and more Parisians had gone missing; more and more of them had been grabbed roughly by the shoulder and shouted at. Héloise and her friends used to whistle the French anthem, "La Marseillaise," as they walked past soldiers on their way to the park, but one of her sister's friends had been taken and held in a jail cell for three days, all because of the simple tune on her lips. Now Héloise grabbed Marie's hand tightly as they walked past soldiers, yanking her along the road and reminding her to keep her eyes down.

Marie scowled. "I'm not a child."

"Thirteen-year-olds are fully grown, then? Must have missed that," he teased.

"You and Héloise," said Marie, rolling her eyes. "Acting as if you're so much older than me."

"We *are*." His eyes were serious once again. "And besides, I'm saying it because it's true. It doesn't matter how old you are, it doesn't matter who your parents are; it doesn't matter where you go to school or work or eat your supper. They're out for blood these days. No talk like that, do you hear me?"

"Fine."

"Good," he said, his bright grin reappearing. He reached into his pocket and pulled out half of a crumbling croissant. "It's the best I could do."

Marie gobbled it instantly. She didn't care that it had been in his pocket, or that it was probably left over from some German. It was the best thing she'd eaten in days.

"Happy birthday, Marie," he said quietly. "May this year be different than the last."

Marie pulled her shawl around herself tightly. The snow was coming; she could smell it in the wind. She picked up her pace and hurried down Rue de Vivienne, toward her sister. Toward where she belonged.

October, present day

PENNY WAS BEGINNING to get the feeling she'd never belong in Paris.

She'd wanted a to-go coffee from the café next door, which she wasn't *technically* allowed to drink. But the barista had looked at her like she'd ordered a McDonald's cheeseburger from a five-star restaurant, the kind Dad's old boss used to take him to.

"We don't have *takeaway*." Her voice dripped with snootiness. "You'll have to go to *Starbucks*." She said it the way you might say "You'll have to dig through the trash." Penny had hurried out, embarrassed, certain that the cool-looking girl behind her in line was laughing at her with the barista the second the door shut behind her.

One year, she kept reminding herself. One measly year. Then she could be back home, with her house that didn't make weird old-building noises and her Java Cat coffee shop. She scrolled her phone, looking at pictures of Rosalie and Erin living their best lives together. After the coffee failure, she'd decided to partake in her second-favorite hobby after painting: lying in bed and thinking about how much she hated the whole entire world.

But she was starting to get a little bored of staring at her phone and moping, if she was being honest. And hungry. Her brothers had gone off with a group of friends they'd made already. Their parents had showed them some kind of Facebook group of foreigners living in Paris and, all of a sudden, they had ridiculously full social calendars. Dad was holed up at a café—with a *real* coffee mug, not a to-go cup, apparently—sending emails and Zooming clients, convincing them that they could become the best version of themselves. Dad was a corporate trainer, and he had a never-ending supply of optimism, whether it was for the CEOs who hired him for leadership training or in his firm belief that Penny would, eventually, fall in love with Paris.

"Penny?" Mom asked, sticking her head into the yellow room. "I have to go out."

"Where?" she asked, trying to sound uninterested.

Mom actually looked kind of excited as she tied her long dark hair back in a ponytail. "Art emergency, believe it or not." Mom's new job had been busy—Penny felt like she barely saw her. Her mother's fellowship was focused on art history research, which meant she was always at the institute, poring over old documents. But she was also teaching a course about Romantic art, and all the prep work, paper grading, and lesson planning took up any free moment she had.

"What kind?"

"Some construction team stumbled on a painting. They're asking me to go help identify what it is. It was tucked inside a *wall*, believe it or not."

"A wall?" Penny sat up. Mysterious paintings behind a wall? Like some kind of movie? "Why are they asking *you*?"

Mom raised an eyebrow. "I'm an expert in art history, am I not? Plus, the head of the program's on vacation. I answered the phone. You coming or what? Maybe we can get some lunch after, if I have time."

It was like Old Mom had bubbled up to the surface, ready to drop everything and take Penny on an adventure.

She grabbed her bag.

Mom sprang for an Uber, since it was only the two of them. Penny watched the streets of Paris fly by through the window as the driver zoomed between cars and down alleyways. Her parents had been trying to get them all used to the Metro, but the maps were confusing, and they often wound up far from where they wanted to be.

Paris was always so chaotic. It was one of the things that made living there feel almost impossible to imagine, even as she did it. Penny missed her quiet street. She missed Rosalie. And mostly she missed her painting teacher, Mrs. Marley. She missed her in the way you miss someone you know you might never see again, a sinking feeling that wrapped itself around her heart and squeezed.

Art had always been what Penny and her mom had in common. While her brothers threw themselves into soccer, Penny had watercolors and oil pastels. Trying to get a ball into a net was her idea of a nightmare, to be honest. And sue her: She didn't get the point. Woo-hoo, you won a sportsball tournament. Here's a trophy. Game's over.

With art, you could create something that would last for years; it could be there long after you were gone and everyone had forgotten the sound of your voice. It could be displayed in a museum, like the ones they passed now in their Uber, for centuries to come. People could look at it and feel hope or sadness or wonder. They'd try to interpret how you were feeling when you made it, in an attempt to understand what you thought was beautiful. Maybe they'd see a little slice of the creator, of *you*, right there on the paper. They'd feel like they *knew* you, even though they'd never met you.

But, hey. Mason's soccer trophies *were* pretty shiny.

Mom had brought her to Mrs. Marley when Penny asked to quit ballet in the fourth grade. It wasn't that she hated ballet; it was that she was tired of it. The same floor exercises, the same barre—there wasn't any *freedom* in it. Everything was the same, the same, the same. You couldn't even wear a bow in your hair at dance class because you were supposed to be one little soldier in a line of ballerinas. The goal was blending in, but Penny had never liked taking orders or fading into the background.

"You can't just sit around after school," her mother insisted, which had kind of bugged Penny. Why not? Plenty of kids just sat around after school. Mom herself, according to Nana, had just sat around after school. But Penny's parents were the kind of people who were always worried she was going to come home one day and announce she wanted to be a YouTube star or start live-streaming her video games or something.

"What do you love to do?" Dad had asked. "You don't have to like sports or dance. You just need to find your *thing.* Your passion! What lights Penny Marks's heart on fire?"

"I don't have *a thing*," Penny said, rolling her eyes. Dad's main job was getting people pumped up to hit their goals at work. He brought the same energy to coaching the boys' soccer teams and parenting his stubbornly unathletic daughter.

"What about drawing?" Mom asked quietly. "You're always doodling." Mom had studied art history at the University of Wisconsin a million years ago, but she had been spending her days taking care of Penny and her brothers and sometimes teaching art classes online to homeschool co-ops. Her biggest dream was to get to return to UW as a professor. She also wrote articles online for art magazines, particularly on the history of a few lesser-known paintings, and some of them had gotten a lot of attention from important people in the art world. Penny knew Mom had never wanted to push her or her brothers into art just because she loved it. But it was true—Penny *did* like to doodle. And art was something she could actually see herself doing every day and not getting bored.

"Fine," she'd said, trying to pretend she didn't notice the excitement hovering behind her mom's eyes.

Mrs. Marley was . . . old. Not, like, *elderly*, but she'd seen some things, that was for sure. She'd been Mom's middle school art teacher, and she still taught at Fernridge Falls Middle, in addition to hosting private lessons in her home.

"There's no one I'd rather have her learn from," Mom insisted, when Dad suggested they maybe look at the university or something more formal. "She's the best of the best."

Going to Mrs. Marley's was like walking into a fairy's woodland cottage. Her house was an arch of brown-and-white pillars, nestled just behind a tangle of wildflowers and overgrown raspberry bushes. Her garden seemed to spring from the earth; a mythical home in the middle of a bustling campus town. The first time Penny had cautiously walked in, there'd been music playing, the soft symphony of chamber songs bursting through the airy kitchen.

"There you are," the woman said, with a gentle smile. She was surrounded by thick piles of paper, jars of water, and paints of every color. Her fingers were stained with ink and paint, and she was wearing cargo pants with a hole at the knee. She smiled at Penny as if she'd been waiting just for her.

From then on, Mrs. Marley's house was her favorite place to be. Whether she was frustrated at how dull school was (sometimes), bored with her friends' weird internet obsessions (often), or annoyed by her brothers (daily), Penny could carve a little space that was all hers.

Mrs. Marley demonstrated different tactics but never touched Penny's paintings—so she could make every painting completely her own. Penny learned everything from watercolor technique to shaping and shadow. She went through enough sketch paper and graphite pencils to fill their garage. Art lessons had always helped Penny just get things *out*: out of her brain, out of her heart, out of her fingertips, and onto a piece of paper.

"You are special, Miss Marks," Mrs. Marley would say, her fingers running across Penny's pictures. "You have talent, and I don't say that to everyone. I said it to your mother, though, and I'll say it to you."

When Penny got to sixth grade, moving from elementary school to middle school, Mrs. Marley became her art teacher there too. She loved feeling extra sparkly in class—sure, Mrs. Marley might be complimenting Owen's papier-mâché owl or Daniela's ceramic ladybug. But Penny knew *she* was *special*.

Mom loved Penny's paintings. She'd hang them everywhere—the fridge, her office, Penny's very own bulletin board. She said she wanted to be surrounded by beauty, and she treated Penny's shabby landscapes as if they were painted by Van Gogh. Mom never acted like Penny was playing around with stickers and glitter glue. She took art seriously—especially when it was created by her daughter.

Penny couldn't exactly remember when it was that painting class had changed. It was like falling asleep. You were right on the edge, all cozy and tucked in, and the next thing you know you're blinking awake to the obnoxious ring of an alarm clock.

It had just started to seem—silly. Or *dumb*, kind of. So much had happened, hadn't it? That year, with the president and the wars and the fires and the angry people on TV. Rosalie, her best friend, joined Global Leaders and spent all of her time after school making pamphlets and signing petitions. The most Penny could contribute was writing PERIOD POVERTY STATISTICS or HOW TO HELP END CLIMATE CHANGE BEFORE IT'S TOO LATE across the top of Rosalie's poster boards in her swirly handwriting. Rosalie was very into saving the planet from—well, everything. War and famine and violence and racism and plastic straws. Things were happening and happening and happening, and there was Penny, doing what? Mixing colors to get the perfect shade of pink for her orchid? She'd dip her paintbrush in her water and she'd hear that Jocelyn James on the news, saying that the point of education was to *prepare kids for the workforce.* Saying kids needed to be trained to *contribute to society.* How was this preparing her for *anything*?

And then—well. Mason.

He'd had a sore throat. Mom said it was probably strep. But it got worse, and worse, and suddenly he couldn't turn his head, and then she was being shaken awake in the middle of the night by Matthew, because Mom and Dad and Mason were leaving in an ambulance. She ran out into the dark hallway and saw their outlines—Mom, crying, and Dad, barking into a phone, and Mason, gasping for air. Clutching his throat. She was up all night, waiting for Matthew's phone to ring with updates. And all of that waiting time left her brain wide open, and when your brain is wide open, all kinds of fears flood in. Little fears, like "I don't like being the only one awake in the house." And bigger fears too. Brother-dying fears.

She had painting class the next day. It was a Tuesday. Mom and Dad were still at the hospital—Mason had bacterial meningitis, an infection of the membranes that protected his brain. They couldn't go see him yet. Matthew drove her to Mrs. Marley's house in silence.

She'd been working on a painting of an orchid. Orchids were her mom's favorite flower.

"Penny, are you all right?" Mrs. Marley had asked her quietly. Clearly, something was wrong. But Penny hadn't said what. She simply kept mixing her colors, a deep red and a bright white to get a plush, soft pink.

"Yeah." There was some kind of old music playing in the background, like they were at a jazz club in the time of romantic dinners and Parisian poets or something.

"All right. Try some different brushstrokes, there on the petal, see? If you try and move the brush horizontally instead of just vertically, you might be able to create some texture."

And there—right there.

Penny put her paintbrush down. Her face felt hot.

"Penny, are you sure you're okay? Do you need some—"

"Who cares?" she bit out.

"What?" Mrs. Marley looked shocked. She should look shocked. Penny had never spoken to a teacher like that in her entire life. It was as if Penny had whipped out a bomb and tossed it onto the table.

"Who cares about—*texture*. It's a stupid painting. It's playing around with paintbrushes like we're preschoolers or something, and this is all so dumb. If you think I'm such a bad artist—"

"Penny! Goodness gracious! I'm just trying to help."

"I don't want to do this anyway." Penny grabbed

the painting and crumpled it up, hard. There was oil paint all over her hands. Some splotched down onto the table, and some dampened her art smock.

She ran out of the house for the last time. She ran the entire two miles home, showing up at the front door with sweat dripping down her temples. Matthew was watching a documentary about Egyptian pharaohs on TV.

"Did I forget to come get you? I thought six. Are you done already?" her brother asked, confused.

"Yeah," said Penny. "I'm done."

Mom didn't find out she had quit until over a month later, when Mason was finally home from the hospital with hearing loss and a million pills to take. Mrs. Marley had called her immediately, but with everything going on, it had gotten lost in the shuffle. When Mom learned what had happened, she'd been more upset than she'd let on, Penny knew. But she let Penny take a break, even though Dad thought it was a bad idea. Penny heard them arguing about it one night—Dad saying "give up" and "disappointment" and "so talented" and Mom saying her "own choices" and "give her space" and "see how it goes."

And in art class at school, where Mrs. Marley was trying to make do with a bunch of recycled construction paper and broken colored pencils, scraping by with donated art supplies parents sometimes brought in, things became more and more tense. Mrs. Marley was as kind as ever, but Penny knew that she was a giant disappointment to her. She couldn't believe she'd yelled at her favorite teacher like that.

She hurried through her projects, getting them done for the sake of getting them done instead of putting in any real effort. It was sort of like sledding at the end of winter. The snow was almost gone, snow pants were already packed away, and lumps of dirt were emerging from the hills. What was the point? Jocelyn James sat in on class a couple of times—her daughter, Annabeth, was in Penny's class. Jocelyn would watch from the back corner, lips pursed. And when April came and she was elected to the school board, Mrs. Marley was out of a job.

Fernridge Falls Middle didn't even *have* an art program anymore, even though Mom angrily insisted it was the law. Instead, they got random rotations of substitute teachers who put on movies while kids did their homework, and early in the summer, the school board had passed some referendum that next year, the time that used to go to art class had to go to math.

Well, Penny hated math. But there was a small part of her that got where Jocelyn James was coming from, not that she'd ever tell Mom or Mrs. Marley. Honestly, what *was* the point, of any of it? How was this going to help end world hunger or homelessness or the other billions of things *wrong* with the world? How was this going to stop a disease that could sneak into your brain and almost—

Stop. Sometimes she'd even say it aloud—*Stop!*—when she wanted to stop her thoughts from racing toward where they were racing. What would have happened without that ambulance.

That was what Rosalie thought too. Rosalie, who'd been Penny's best friend since Girl Scouts in kindergarten, when they wore those scratchy blue vests and promised to be honest and fair, friendly and helpful. But ever since Rosalie had joined Fernridge Falls Middle's chapter of Global Leaders, she'd been spending a lot of time with Erin, the Global Leaders president.

Erin Drust was the daughter of Rick Drust, king of auto sales in northeastern Wisconsin. *Rick Drust Is Who You Can Trust.* Erin, who had political stickers on her binder and listened to news podcasts, thought Rosalie hung the moon. They talked about Yemen and Ukraine, while Penny wasn't one-hundred-percent sure what the difference between a senator and a representative was. Before Penny had quit, she'd once told them that she couldn't go to a Global Leaders fundraiser because she had painting class, and she'd seen the she-doesn't-get-it look they passed each other. Like Penny was playing Picasso while they were saving the world.

And maybe she *didn't* get it.

But that didn't mean she didn't miss the feel of a paintbrush between her fingers, or that she didn't wake up in the middle of the night from dreams of attending her own gallery openings.

Penny had thought she could maybe give painting another shot in Paris, away from Rosalie and Erin's judgmental looks. Maybe she'd feel more inspired in the City of Light, the center of incredible art history. A place with much less drama than Fernridge Falls Middle had had, or so she thought. But now they couldn't find a teacher. And Paris had its own issues blaring on the news. Penny was alone. No Yoda to her Luke Skywalker. Just a girl, in a city filled to the brim with art museums but no one who thought she had any talent at all.

Except Mom. But it was Mom's fault she was in Paris in the first place, so she couldn't be an ally, either.

"Here it is," Mom said to the driver, pointing to a gorgeously ornate building on the corner. It crept up toward the sky, the iron gate a lavish design of leaves and flowers, the faded pink popping against the bright blue autumn sky.

Mom thanked the Uber driver, and the two of them ducked out cautiously.

"Are you sure this is the right place?" Penny asked.

Mom glanced at her phone, and back to the building. "Two-two-one-seven Rue de Augustine. I guess we'll find out."

Penny followed her mom inside, through a heavy door. They were smacked in the face with the smell of construction—that, at least, was the same in every country. Sawdust and fresh paint swirled heavily in the air, and grumpy-looking men in overalls ignored them. It was an apartment, though; that much she could tell. There was a bathroom and a kitchen and gutted-out walls.

A woman ran over and immediately started speaking in rapid-fire French to Penny's mom, who tried to respond slowly. The woman sighed in frustration and switched to heavily accented English.

"The owner, she tells me to call an auctioneer. I don't do this! I manage the construction. I don't know auctioneers. She says, 'Get rid of it.' But my father, he knows art, yes? He says to call Institut National d'Histoire de l'Art. And they send me an American?"

Penny glared at the woman, but Mom just smiled. "My French may not sound lovely, but I promise you, I know my art. My supervisor said you found a painting hidden in a wall?"

"Oui," she said, motioning for them to follow her. They stepped carefully over small piles of construction materials and paint cans, walking through a grand hall to the opposite side of a living room.

"The foundation is no good. We need to fix," the woman said. "But we break through the plaster, and . . ." She motioned toward the wall.

Lying there, between the wooden wall frames, was a large painting. It had clearly been rolled up for a while, but now it was unfurled, with duct tape holding the corners to the beams, which Penny knew would horrify Mom. Her mother pulled on some rubber gloves and knelt down to get a better look at the painting. Penny did the same. Once she did, she gasped.

The painting was simple, but clear: a woman looking out a window, the sun barely breaching her face. There was a table just behind her with a bowl of fruit on it, a few spotted bananas and an apple or two. A cat lay curled under the table, sound asleep. Mrs. Marley would have pointed out the way the artist played with the light and the way you could feel the movement as the woman leaned.

As Penny identified the technique—those gentle brushstrokes—she also felt a familiar feeling unlock in the pit of her stomach: the feeling of looking at something that just . . . took your breath away. A feeling you couldn't explain, or put into words, even if she'd tried.

How on earth had something so beautiful wound up in the wall? Not *on* the wall, like a normal painting would be—but *in* the wall. As if someone had hidden it.

Who would want to hide such a beautiful work of art? Who wouldn't want to hang it in their home, having as many people enjoy it as possible? It didn't make any sense.

"Wow." Her mom exhaled. "I'm going to . . . well, I'll need some assistance getting it over to the institute. It's very, very old. Fragile. Lovely. Hold on." Mom stepped back, took a few careful, flashless photos, and then stepped away to make a call, speaking in broken French.

Penny leaned in to get a closer look at the painting, while being careful not to touch the canvas or even breathe too heavily. But as she did, she spotted a small piece of paper lying about a foot away. It was in the dark, behind plaster that hadn't yet been pulled out.

She carefully touched the paper, just barely letting it graze her fingertips. There were smudged French words on it. It could have been left by the construction workers, but something told her it wasn't. She saw a year, in the middle of all of the swirling French words—1944. Maybe this was the note that could identify exactly who the painting had belonged to and why it had wound up where it had.

The wheels started spinning in her head. This note could be the key to everything. She turned to tell her mom what she'd found.

"Penny?" Mom suddenly called from the next room before Penny could get a word out. "Dad's coming to get you in an Uber, honey. I've got a few people from work that need to see this, and it's going to take all my attention."

"But—"

Hadn't she said they'd maybe have time for lunch? She pictured herself showing her mom the letter, and the two of them poring over it together. Mom could help her translate it, and they could solve this mystery, and—

"He said he'd take you for ice cream. You haven't been to Berthillon yet! It's supposed to be the best ice cream in all of Paris."

"I can . . ."

But Mom was speaking in French again, into her phone.

Fury wrapped its way around Penny's heart. Her mother, getting rid of her—*again*. Pushing her off. Putting work first. Putting *herself* first. The New Mom was back, the one with the fancy job and things to do and places to be and people to see. Old Mom—the one who took Penny on spontaneous adventures to find paintings hidden in walls—had vanished.

And maybe it was that fury. Maybe it was the rage of having to be in a place she didn't want to be. Maybe it was the knowledge that she'd never be able to create anything half as beautiful as that painting; that the gap between what she wanted to make and what she was able to make was a mile wide. Maybe any of these reasons—or a thousand others—was why Penny took that note and slid it into the pocket of her jeans as quickly as she could without being seen.

December 1943

AS QUICKLY AS she could without being seen, Marie tucked the note from Clarisse into her pocket. She'd read it quickly—if Monsieur Bassot confiscated it, both she and Clarisse would have to write lines until their fingers were sore.

Papa said the Allies are coming.

Clarisse wasn't the only one who thought so. Those were the words on everyone's lips at school. Marie could hear it, passed around the hallways like a secret. That was why the Nazis were so angry; that was why they were feeling so spiteful. That was why you couldn't look at a Nazi wrong, walk past a Nazi wrong, speak in front of a Nazi wrong. Every move now held danger.

Paris, Marie felt, had grown both more and less crowded than ever. It was emptier; so many people were gone. Everyone's father had been sent to work and everyone's neighbor had been taken to jail and everyone's cousin had escaped the chill of Paris, finding a forbidden way to the countryside. But at the same time, everything seemed *fuller*. There might have been fewer desks at school, but every café was jam-packed with people who were desperate for warmth. Everyone squished together in the long lines that Héloïse sent Marie to stand in for rationed food. Where you could get a fresh ration card. How you could repair the hole punched in your card to get another helping. Who had the best black market bread; where you could find black market chicken.

Chicken! Marie *dreamed* of chicken. What a silly thing to dream of, but she really did. Last night she'd dreamed that Maman had brought a roast chicken to the table, shimmering with juice and surrounded by vegetables. Vegetables Marie had once complained about eating but would now give anything to taste. When she brought a forkful to her mouth, though, it turned to ash just as it touched her lips.

Marie claimed a stomachache and left before her final classes. She couldn't listen to Monsieur Bassot drone on for another minute. And it wasn't a lie—she did have a stomachache, the same aching hunger she'd had for years. She stopped at the café window before heading home, but Adrien shook his head at her through the window, an apology in his eyes. Nothing to spare today. Nothing to share.

When she got to the apartment, she heard quiet chattering in the kitchen stop suddenly. It was Héloise, home early from a day at the Ritz, and her new friend Jeanne. Like Jeanne d'Arc, in more ways than one.

Héloise's new friend was the type to live a life of adventure too; with the right armor and sword she seemed like she could turn the entire world around. Marie didn't know very much about her—Jeanne had only become friends with Héloise in the past month. But she had beautiful brown hair and always wore a stylish scarf tied just so around her neck. And she smiled as if she had secrets.

"You're home from work early," said Marie, dropping her bag on the floor.

Héloise raised her eyebrows at her. "You're home from school early."

"Classes were canceled," she lied, easy as anything "No heat."

"I had Alexine cover my shift," said Héloise. "My feet are aching, and Madame Auzello sent me home."

Marie had a feeling Héloise was lying too. They

stared at each other for a moment, a sister standoff. But what could she say? Everyone had things they didn't want to share. It was none of her business.

"Come, Marie," said Jeanne with a smile. She patted the chair next to her. "Sit with us. What did you learn today?"

"Nothing, I'm sure," muttered Héloise. "She daydreamed and doodled until she skipped out of class."

Marie rolled her eyes as she sat, pulling off her shawl. "My sister worries too much."

"She worries just enough," proclaimed Jeanne. "An education is important. You're a lucky girl."

"Jeanne d'Arc didn't go to school," said Marie. She grabbed Héloise's small cup and took a sip of the coffee in it. It wasn't real coffee, of course, just roasted barley and acorns. It was as gross as ever, but it warmed her stomach. "She fought for France."

"Well, we'll need to get you a proper uniform," said Jeanne, laughing. She rose and began to gather some of her things, effortlessly retying her scarf.

"Enough of that," snapped Héloise. "Don't put ideas into her head, or I'll find her traipsing about Paris with a shield."

"Oh, relax, Héloise," said Jeanne, patting her hand. "I was only kidding. I find Marie's spunk admirable, that's all. I'd better be off, anyway."

There was a knock at the door—two quick, one slow. Adrien.

"Stay," said Marie. "Adrien's here, and he'll tell us stories of the stupid haricots verts at work." Some girls at school had started calling the Germans green beans, for their skinniness and ugly green uniforms. Marie found it hilarious.

But Jeanne simply smiled. "I have my own work to do, I'm afraid." Jeanne ran deliveries for shops around the city and was always flying down the street on her bicycle.

Adrien poked his head through the door. "Anyone home? I'm desperate for the sound of a voice that isn't barking at me for more wine."

"Happy to oblige," said Héloise, raising her cup with a smile. Jeanne leaned down and planted a kiss hard on Marie's head before breezing out the door past Adrien without so much as a bonjour. For some reason, the two of them didn't seem to like each other very much.

"Sit," said Marie, pulling out a chair for her almost-brother. He flopped into it and groaned.

"My feet are killing me," he said.

"So are mine," confessed Marie.

"I'm sorry," Héloise said, wincing. "I know you need new shoes. . . ."

"Oh, these are fine," said Marie quickly, trying to cover up her mistake. She hated admitting things to Héloise that she knew her sister couldn't fix. Even if they had money for new shoes, which they didn't, the soles of any shoes available were made of wood since the Germans had taken all of the leather. The wood-soled shoes were ridiculously loud, almost as loud as the boots of the Germans. Marie would much prefer pinched toes.

"How was work?" Héloise asked Adrien. "I was just about to make us some pasta for supper, if you can stay." Marie knew that would mean smaller portions, but she also loved the way Adrien's company seemed to warm the entire apartment.

Adrien sighed. "Thanks. It was . . . not so good. You know my coworker, Emile? He speaks German. Had a German nanny. Sometimes he tells me what he overhears the soldiers saying. Today they were going off about arresting a boy who had written *V*s all over their propaganda signs." Marie knew the signs—lines and lines of them, boasting about the friendliness between the Germans and the French, begging any Frenchmen who hadn't yet been forced to work in Germany to do so voluntarily, bragging about the German victories across Europe. If you believed the girls at school, most of those victories were twisted; Clarisse said her father listened to the BBC on a secret radio every night; they reported that the Germans were low on food and weapons.

"*V* for *victoire*," Marie said with a smile. She loved seeing the *V*s that vandals scribbled across posters and in shop windows. Sometimes she and her friends would even flash each other *V*s with their fingers if they passed one another in the street.

"That was brave of him," said Héloise quietly.

"Yes, well. Brave and *stupid*," Adrien said, grim-faced. "He was captured and sent away. Sixteen years old. One of the Nazi soldiers said he almost peed himself, and the rest of them laughed."

Marie froze. Captured? For simply writing a letter *V*? But plenty of people did that!

"Adrien," murmured Héloise, glancing at her sister.

"Don't do that," snapped Marie. She *hated* when they did that! Treated her like a child. As if she didn't see the propaganda or hear the boots. As if she didn't see the giant sign draped across the old bookstore: DEUTSCHLAND SIEGT AN ALLEN FRONTEN. Germany is victorious everywhere.

Adrien just sighed. He seemed so defeated—nothing like the Adrien she'd known growing up, who would spin her around while singing "Tick, tock, it's Marie o'clock!" Nothing like the boy who would cross his eyes at her at Mass. Now he was just . . . tired. Tired of Germans and tired of work. Tired of the cloud that the occupation hung over them, thick and gray. There was no trace of the joy that used to permeate his eyes.

Joy—yet another thing the Nazis had stolen.

"I thought the Americans would be here soon," said Marie. "I thought—"

"I think that's why they're so angry," said Adrien, keeping his voice low. The walls were thin. You never knew who could be listening. "They arrest more and more, every day. Things they would have ignored a couple of years ago, they'll toss you in jail for now. That's why you need to be careful, Marie. No little jokes with your friends. Don't even mention the Americans, or anything about the Allies. Just keep your head down."

"You sound like our father," Héloise teased him.

"Your father was right," said Adrien, not a hint of joke in his voice. "It's like the rabbit in his story, right?"

Le Petit Lapin Rose. Marie had read it so many times she could recite it. If she closed her eyes tightly at night, she could hear Papa's rumbling voice reading it to her, doing different sounds for each woodland creature. It was about a small pink rabbit who was too afraid to leave his hutch. There were too many dangers outside—foxes and wolves and snakes. So the rabbit stayed inside, painting his walls. First he painted a rainbow; then a garden scene; then Noah's Ark with all of the animals, two by two; then the night sky. He made his small world beautiful and realized he didn't need to leave his hutch. He had everything he needed.

"Stay hidden in your rabbit hutch. Don't attract attention. Pour the wine and drink the disgusting coffee," said Adrien. "That's what I tell myself, and what you should tell yourselves too."

"I'm sorry you had a hard day," said Héloise sympathetically.

He stared out the window. "Not so hard. You two are safe, and so am I. That's all we can ask for, right now. It's more than most can say."

Marie thought of the horrible morning after the roundup of the Jews, when Sarah and so many others had vanished. The sounds coming from the Vélodrome d'Hiver, where they'd been taken, and the horrible silence that followed once they'd gone. She had sobbed into Héloise's arms for a week.

Adrien was right—she should be grateful she was still in Paris. And at the same time, she felt horrible for thinking so. Her guilt for Sarah and shame for her own self-pity swirled around in her stomach until she felt ill.

"All we can put our hope in is our ability to get through the day," said Adrien.

Héloise reached over and squeezed Marie's shoulder tightly. But it didn't bring her much comfort. In fact, it only made her feel worse.

That Sunday, church was long and dull and cold, like always. Père Maurice droned on and on about carrying the cross of Jesus, and Marie fidgeted in her too-small shoes. She wished they could skip Sunday Mass now that nobody was there to make them go, but Héloise said their parents wouldn't want them to. Marie knew that was true. Maman had loved church—the beautiful windows, the soaring voices singing all together. She said it made her heart light. And Papa believed it was their Catholic duty.

But in a world full of discomforts, she wished they could at least sleep in on Sundays. Marie spent most of Mass picking at the hole in her stockings until Héloise leaned over and pinched her to stop.

"If you think I'll be able to find fabric to mend those, you've lost your mind," her sister whispered.

Afterward, Marie walked home with Adrien and Héloise, dodging the bicycles that sped past them. It was nearly Christmas, but the Advent season hadn't been very cheery for years. She knew there wouldn't be a bûche de Noël; nor would there be any gifts. There wouldn't be a midnight Mass, as it would be breaking the strict curfew in place. There wouldn't even be a fire to warm their hands in front of, at this rate. Ever since the war had started, winters seemed to be responding; they were colder than Marie ever remembered them being. The second year the Nazis were there, it had even snowed enough to go sledding with Héloïse and Papa.

"Halt!" Marie froze, snapping out of her memory of winters past. A German was yelling at a blond young woman, and Marie couldn't understand.

"What do you want?" the woman said sharply.

"Open your bag," the soldier replied, in a hideous attempt at French.

The woman clutched her bag. "I'll do no such thing. You have no right—"

The German yanked the bag out of her hands.

"Hurry, Héloïse," muttered Adrien. "Think of Marie... we need to—"

But her sister was frozen. Marie stared at Héloïse, and Héloïse stared at the man. The people around them paid no attention; they simply pushed past Adrien and the Bonnet sisters as if their next errand was the most important thing in the world. Just another daily happening in Paris. Just another horror.

"What is this?" the German barked, pulling out what looked like a newspaper to Marie. *Défense de la France.*

"None of your business," the woman snapped.

"Come with me," responded the soldier, his voice thick with nails and warning.

And of course the woman would go. She would, because she wasn't foolish. Because the Nazis had been there for over three years by this point, and she had to know that denying was dangerous. You did what the Germans said. You stayed in your rabbit hutch.

But a person can be so broken down that they snap, like the acorns to make ersatz coffee. When you've lost your dignity and your coal and your choices, you have nothing upon which to steady your feet. Marie knew that, and so did the woman. The woman cocked her head back and spat, hard, into the face of the soldier. A giant wad of spit rolled down his cheek. Héloise's hand flew to her mouth.

"Héloise!" whispered Adrien frantically.

For a moment, it seemed as if the only people on the street were the three of them, and the Nazi and the defiant blond woman. The whizzing bicycles faded into the background. A black Mercedes, driven by more Germans, sped past. Marie barely noticed it.

The Nazi soldier reached for his gun.

Adrien suddenly grabbed Marie, spinning her around, and pressed her face into his chest. He held her head there so she couldn't see. She couldn't pull away, even if she tried. She breathed in the familiar smell of Adrien's threadbare jacket. Her own little hutch.

Crack.

Not the sound of a gunshot, but the sound of metal hitting skull. The slump of a body, the chaos of a bag being spilled open. A few coins, rolling into the gutter. Marie could not see it, but she could *hear* it, every slight noise in a jumble of sound.

Adrien was yanking her, still holding her tightly, and now Héloise was following them, and they were running. There were no shouts. No screams. No acknowledgment of what they had just witnessed. Just the harsh *thump-thump-thump* of their too-small shoes hitting the pavement. She breathed in fits and spurts, the icy air a shock to her throat.

But just as they turned the corner to Rue de Vivienne, Marie was able to turn. She saw the lump in the street, the blond hair fanned out among the cobblestones. She saw a navy-blue coat, growing wet with blood. And she saw the soldier, walking away.

They got home and hurried up the stairs, running as fast as they could. Their footsteps sounded like a stampede on the wooden staircase. Someone called out a greeting to Adrien; he ignored them. The three of them burst into the apartment. Héloise was shaking so badly she could barely walk.

"That . . . that . . ." Marie didn't have the words.

"It's okay," Adrien said, almost whispering. "You're okay. She shouldn't have had that newspaper. Spitting—what was she *thinking*?"

What was *she* thinking? What was the *woman* thinking? What about the *German*? What about—

Héloise still hadn't said a word. She stared out the window.

"Héloise," Adrien said to her softly. Then a bit louder. "*Héloise*. Are you all right?"

The three of them sat in silence for a minute. Marie wished more than anything that they had taken a different route home, or walked faster. She knew this much: She might not have seen the woman get hit, but she'd be seeing it in her mind's eye for a very, very long time.

Finally her sister turned around. "I'm fine," she said flatly. "But I need to go out."

"For what?" Marie asked her.

"For some bread."

"*Now?* He won't have a single thing left. We'll queue up tomorrow morning, like always," said Marie, confused. If you wanted any chance at getting bread, you had to be in line hours before the baker actually opened, ration card at the ready.

"For a walk, then," snapped Héloise. "I need to clear my mind. To get some fresh air."

"Héloise, you're still shaking. And it's so cold. Sit," said Adrien. "Let me make you a coffee."

"I don't want a coffee, and besides, we can't waste the coal to heat the water," she said. "I'm going out. I need a minute. I'll be careful. *Le Petit Lapin Rose*, okay? I won't talk to any wolves. Stay with Marie, will you?"

"I don't need—" Marie insisted.

"Of course," promised Adrien.

"I'll be back," said Héloise. And she went right back out the door, letting it slam behind her.

Marie and Adrien just sat in more silence. That blood. That blond hair—

"Remember when we were small?" Adrien asked. "And I would swing you upside down?"

"Tick, tock, Marie o'clock," said Marie. Her voice sounded hollow.

"What would we do right now?" said Adrien quietly. "If the Germans weren't here?"

Marie squeezed her eyes shut tight. Otherwise she might cry. It was a game they played, sometimes. Daydreaming about a past that might never return.

Sometimes it cheered her up, imagining that one day they'd have their world back again.

"Go to the movies," she finally said. "At the Grand Rex cinema." Their favorite theater, which was closed to Parisians now, so the Germans could enjoy their own films in peace.

"Buy some croissants," said Adrien. "Chocolate-filled ones."

"And picnic by the Seine," Marie said. "With strawberry ice cream."

"And go to the Louvre." There was no point in visiting now, although it was technically open. Almost all of the art had been smuggled out before the war to protect it, if you believed such things. The painting of Jeanne d'Arc that Maman had loved so—where had it gone? Would she ever see it again?

"With Papa," Marie whispered.

Yes, sometimes the game cheered her. But other times, it made her desolate. She hadn't realized what she'd had when she'd had it. She hadn't realized that every single day had been a gift until every single day walked her further toward despair.

Adrien reached to hug her, and she let him, thinking of croissants, and cinemas, and strawberry ice cream, cold and sweet.

October, present day

PENNY DIDN'T LOOK at the letter that day, when her dad picked her up and took her for a scoop of strawberry ice cream. (One thing she and her dad could agree on—the French didn't appreciate the proper size of an ice cream scoop. She had to order a triple to get what would have been a kid's size in America.)

She didn't look at it the day after that, even though she got incredibly bored listening to her homeschool co-op science teacher drone on about rock formations.

She didn't even look at it the day after *that*, when Mom came home from work all stressed out because the press had heard about the painting and there were all these stories being written about the mysterious work of art found in the wall.

No, Penny kept the letter folded, like something exciting to help her get through the day. It reminded her of the old feeling she'd have when she was halfway through an oil portrait. She hated to finish it, because it meant the process of creating it was over. It would be the thing that kept her going through excruciatingly dull pre-algebra classes or yet another soccer tournament—daydreaming about how she could take her art to the next level. Which shade of yellow was just right, or which type of paintbrush would give the brushstroke effect she was hoping for.

But on that fourth morning, a perfect autumn morning in Paris, something changed.

Penny was FaceTiming Rosalie. Scratch that—she was *finally* FaceTiming Rosalie. It had been ridiculously hard to find a time to connect, since Penny was eight hours ahead; she was usually in bed by the time Rosalie was done with school. But tonight she couldn't sleep, and figured she'd spontaneously try her luck. Her parents were watching some documentary in the living room and her brothers were all holed up studying, allegedly, although she'd heard Matthew talking to his girlfriend earlier and Mason making obnoxious kissing noises at him.

"And then Erin's dad took us backstage," Rosalie was saying all excitedly. Now that Penny was across the world, Erin's path to best friendship was clear. Apparently, a Caleb Evers concert with backstage passes had sealed the deal. "We got a *picture* with Caleb!"

"I know. I saw online," said Penny. "He's not as tall as I thought he'd be."

"Really? Anyway, it was amazing. He was giving ten percent of show proceeds to help combat climate change. His new song, 'Hotter than the Earth'? It's all about fighting global warming! We're gonna discuss the lyrics at Global Leaders next week."

Penny tried not to roll her eyes. She highly doubted Caleb Evers, who had a private jet, was that concerned about greenhouse gas emissions.

"I wish you'd been there," said Rosalie.

Penny gave her best attempt at a fake smile. "Yeah. Me too."

"You know, I'm sure there are Global Leaders homeschooling chapters," said Rosalie. "Now that you don't have to waste your time in gym or pre-algebra."

"I still have to take math," Penny reminded her.

"Not with Mr. Grendell's bad breath over your shoulder. And you quit painting, right? Honestly, this could be an opportunity. You could be making a real difference! France is at the forefront of nuclear energy!"

"Maybe," said Penny half-heartedly.

"Anyway. My life is totally lame compared to the

adventures *you're* having, I bet. Have you seen the Eiffel Tower yet?"

"Yup. It's cool." It was actually just a giant metal thing, and Penny had no idea why everyone was so excited about it, but yeah, whatever. Just as cool as backstage passes to a Caleb Evers concert on a school night.

"Awesome. Hey, I've gotta run—Erin and I are going to a movie. Au revoir!"

Penny just sat there for a minute after Rosalie had hung up, staring at her phone. It was exactly what she'd been afraid of. Her entire life was just . . . moving along without her. Nobody even felt the hole she'd left behind—Erin had just scooted right over to take her place. Mrs. Marley had probably taken on new students too. She had all the time in the world, now that she wasn't at Fernridge Falls Middle, or teaching Penny how to blend her greens and blues. The planet was still turning, and here was Penny, a world away with zero friends or hobbies or talent. She didn't have a role in her mom's fancy new life in Paris, and she didn't have a role waiting for her back home. She was just floating, like the crunchy leaves outside cascading down from the trees. Dead weight.

Well. She did have *one* exciting thing. One teensy, tiny, letter-shaped adventure.

Penny locked her door—you could never take chances with two brothers. She still remembered the time Mason had gotten mad at her about something at dinner and started reciting sections from her journal that he'd read. She'd kept her room on level-ten lockdown ever since.

Penny pulled out the yellowed sheet of drawing paper from the corner of her bedside table drawer where she'd gently tucked it. She unfolded it slowly, holding up her phone to Google Translate the shaky French handwriting. Then she took a deep breath, zoomed in, and started to read.

Jeanne,

By the time you read this, Héloïse and I will be gone. Adrien was able to secure us papers and we're starting a new life. We can't end 1944 the way we began it.

I know that you might be angry, but I beg you to understand. I made a promise to my sister, remember? I swore she would never lose me.

We will always remember you, and all you did for us and for France.

Love,
Marie Bonnet

Penny read it again, from the beginning. What *was* this? Some kind of goodbye letter. All Jeanne did for France? Who was Jeanne?

Penny folded up the letter and placed it back in her drawer. She quickly pulled on her coziest pair of sweatpants and flopped down into her bed, opening up her laptop. If Jeanne had done something big for France, she'd surely be on the internet, right? But *Jeanne + France* only brought up a ton of articles on St. Joan of Arc. She tried again with *Jeanne in France 1944* and came up with a bunch of websites in French.

Marie Bonnet in France 1944 and *Héloise in France 1944* were similarly unhelpful. But there was one more name to try: *Adrien in France 1944*.

Well, first of all, there was a comedy movie released in France in the 1940s called *Adrien*. Not helpful. But the very next link was a Wikipedia page for French Resistance fighters.

The French Resistance? Like, the people who fought to free France from the Germans? Creepy.

She clicked on it, but there were *tons* of names. Almost a thousand. She got to fifteen different Adriens before she stopped counting. Could one of these be the Adrien the letter mentioned?

Someone tried her doorknob before sighing and knocking.

"Pen," her mom called, "you know how I feel about locked doors."

Penny slammed her laptop shut and shoved it under her bed before hopping up to let her mom in.

"Brother precautions," she explained, opening the door. Mom just raised an eyebrow.

"We're not a locked-door family," she said. "You can remind them to knock, you know."

"You remind them every night not to burp at the table, but it's not like it *works*."

"Well, listen. I came with cool news."

Penny rolled her eyes and laid back down on her bed. Mom sat next to her and rubbed her head, gently pushing the hair from her forehead.

"I wanted to tell you before I went to bed that we had that historian come check out the painting we found." Penny's heart warmed a bit—she loved how her mom said *they* found it, as if they had just stumbled upon it together.

"She analyzed the canvas and oil. It turns out there were initials in the corner—D.O."

"D.O.?"

"Delphine Ollier. She was a middling painter in the 1800s, specializing in portraits and—"

"Mom. There was nothing *middling* about that painting!" Penny's heart raced the way it always did when she felt the need to defend something she loved. Penny didn't know how to speak French or any Caleb Evers lyrics or what, exactly, the difference was between a prime minister and a president. But she knew beauty when she saw it. She had an artist's mind, and it still hadn't been squished out of her, even after everything had crumbled. And Penny knew what all people who love beautiful things know: that when you see something that makes you feel like that, you should share it. Not stuff it behind a wall.

"I don't mean middling, like, *not that good*! I mean middling, like, never made it big. There's some evidence that she knew Edgar Degas. She applied to the École des Beaux-Arts, but they didn't accept women."

Penny groaned. Classic. Art history was riddled with stories of great female artists who weren't allowed to study or succeed the way they deserved—the way so many of the male artists got to. It drove her nuts—all the paintings the world had never gotten to see because of a bunch of grumpy men and their *rules*. All the art that got snuffed out like a dying campfire because someone saw who made it and thought they had the wrong body parts. Like periods and the ability to understand color composition were mutually exclusive.

"I know," Mom said with an eyeroll. "But—some beauty still came from that, didn't it? She ended up copying paintings at the Louvre. Lots of women used to do that and sell their copies. You even had to have a special pass."

"That's so unfair."

"I know, Pen, but artists throughout history have had to struggle to find a way to make their art. Kind of like finding an art teacher who will teach you in English when your mom drags you halfway across the world."

"Me and Delphine," muttered Penny. "Two of a kind."

"Anyway. She ended up working under Thomas Couture, who *did* champion a lot of female artists, and she eventually had a few paintings accepted to the Paris Salon. Isn't it remarkable how, throughout history, people have been creating paintings, even under the worst circumstances? I mean—talk about impressive. The barriers she had to overcome. It's as necessary as eating, to some people. As *breathing*." Penny remembered when she had felt like that. Kind of. "She didn't become really well-known until after she died in 1905."

"So how did one of her paintings end up in the wall?" Penny asked.

"Well," Mom admitted, "that part, I'm afraid I have no idea about. But to have discovered a missing Delphine Ollier—it's really exciting, Penny. It's a *huge* find in the art world. And you helped make it happen!"

"I rode along in the Uber."

"Penelope Rose. The *point* is, I'm glad you were there with me. We're trying to find out who the painting belonged to, but . . ." Mom sighed. "It's really hard. We can't tell how long it's been back there."

Penny opened her mouth to tell her mom that she knew exactly how long it had been back there. Since 1944, just like the note said. But Mom kept going.

"Now, if we could discover *that*," said Mom, "we'd be big deals, Pen!"

Penny cracked a smile.

Big deals. Her mom already was a big deal. To the institute of art, at least. But—not to UW. Not to the place she'd always wanted to be a big deal, before she'd had to quit to take care of Penny and her brothers.

"You look exhausted, kid," Mom said. "Sleep in tomorrow. You don't have your math tutor until ten, right?"

Penny nodded. Mom leaned down and gave her a kiss on the forehead before turning out her light. Outside, a hard wind blew, and the window rattled like ghosts. Penny closed her eyes, willing sleep to come.

January 1944

THE CLASSROOM WINDOWS rattled so loudly that Marie nearly jumped out of her skin. Monsieur Bassot continued to drone on, as if he didn't notice that all of the students in front of him were shivering so badly they could hardly hold pencils. Their fingertips were numb and their toes ached.

Christmas had come and gone with little fanfare, just as Marie had expected it to. Héloise had sketched her a picture of the two of them strolling along the Seine, as a gift, and Marie kept it on her dresser. Adrien had managed to snatch a few leftover desserts from the café, and they ate them greedily, trying to forget that they probably had bits of German spittle on them.

December had turned the corner into January, and although Marie didn't know how it could possibly get colder, it did. The cold seeped into her bones, wetting and weighing them down. She knew that of all of the miserable parts of the war, the cold was one she'd remember the longest.

Both Adrien and Héloise were working as much as they could, desperate for their weekly paycheck. The only way to get coal or meat was to buy it from someone who knew someone who knew someone—a complicated web of people with connections they didn't really have. But while Adrien looked so tired that he barely waved to Marie through the café window, Héloise almost seemed to have a spring in her step. Marie hated going to sleep all alone in the apartment so many nights, but whatever was cheering her sister, she appreciated it. Nothing was worse than Héloise Bonnet in a mood.

Sometimes she even appreciated the quiet. With Sarah gone, all Marie had was Clarisse. And that girl could *talk*. Marie often wanted to tell her to be more careful, but she didn't want to sound like Adrien. Clarisse went on and on about her father's radio, the way *her* family wasn't collaborating but was pushing back against the Germans. Clarisse's father hadn't had to go to Germany to work since he was a doctor. They even got to keep their car. According to Clarisse, he was practically leading the Resistance. Clarisse's voice filled with venom when she talked about their classmate Chloé, whose family owned the café where Adrien worked. How dare they serve Germans? How dare they let them hold meetings there? But her rambling and ranting annoyed Marie. What was Chloé's father supposed to *do*? Say no and be hauled off, letting Chloé starve? Was *Adrien* a collaborator, just for trying to keep warm and make a living and work somewhere where he could get extra food for Héloise and Marie? Or Héloise, for working at the Ritz, which was positively overrun with Germans? Of course not.

In a hushed whisper between arithmetic problems, Marie told her about what she'd seen with Adrien and Héloise a few weeks ago—the woman with the blond hair—and Clarisse just nodded confidently, as if nothing Marie had to say was of interest.

"*Défense de la France* is a Resistance newspaper," Clarisse told her. "Of course my father *always* reads it."

Ah, yes. Her father, who probably had a personal line to Charles de Gaulle, the French general on the radio who encouraged French citizens to rise up against the Germans. Marie wished for the millionth time that Sarah was there to roll her eyes with.

That very afternoon, Héloise burst into the house, clutching her raggedy brown bag. That very afternoon— what a coincidence, wasn't it? Like something you'd read in book. But that's how it went, sometimes. Coincidences. Happenstance. God, Maman would have said. Luck, Papa would have pushed back. Marie didn't know what she thought. Probably a combination of all of the above.

"I need to go," Héloise said. "Another shift opened up at the hotel, and I need to take it. You'll be all right tonight? I'll send Adrien to check in on you."

"I don't need checking in on. Where were you?"

"Just out for a walk. I needed some fresh air. There's bread for dinner." Héloise dropped her bag quickly and hurried to her room to change into her chambermaid uniform. The bag fell open, and a few papers spilled out as her sister slammed the bedroom door.

Marie glanced over at where the bag had fallen—

—and there it was.

A corner of a newspaper. A newspaper? What on earth would Héloise be doing with a newspaper? She didn't read the news. Besides, the news was all propaganda now. The Germans crowing about their victories. You might as well burn it to keep warm, which they did on occasion.

Across the top: a *D*.

Marie walked over as silently as she could—the creaky floors of their old apartment didn't allow her much silence—and reached forward, just barely pulling out the paper to see it.

Défense de la France.

She ripped her hand back as if she'd been burned. A Resistance newspaper? Héloise had a *Resistance newspaper*?

Didn't she know what could *happen*? Didn't she remember what they'd seen?

A thousand emotions flashed through her. Horror. Anger, that Héloise was keeping this from her. As if Marie wouldn't understand or couldn't handle it! As if she was keeping a secret. But then—

Pride.

Her sister, reading a Resistance newspaper? Her cautious, careful Héloise? Héloise was the one who looked both ways four times before crossing the street. Even now, when there were hardly any cars in all of Paris! She, along with Adrien, constantly reminded Marie to mind the Germans, to avoid eye contact, to step out of the way. She sat silently in church. She'd always done her schoolwork on time, and had never missed a shift at the Ritz. Who lived like that? Héloise Bonnet did, that's who.

But here she was. With a completely illegal newspaper.

Her very own Héloise.

Héloise, who was now coming. Marie quickly shoved the corner of the paper back in the bag and hurriedly returned to the table. Héloise opened the door, and the two of them froze.

Marie wanted to say something. She wanted to tell her she was happy for her, that she—

"Were you in my bag?" Héloise asked carefully.

Marie quickly shook her head. "Of course not."

She'd lied to her sister. It wasn't the first time, and it wouldn't be the last.

But this time, she didn't know *why* she was lying. She just felt like it would cause more trouble than it was worth. Héloise would be furious; maybe she'd even burn the paper before Marie got a chance to look more closely at it. Perhaps she'd ask Héloise about it later. Maybe her sister was trying to figure out a way to help Paris. Maybe . . . maybe they could do it together.

Héloise walked over to the bag carefully, picking it up and clutching it to her chest.

"What are you hiding in there?" Marie said, trying to sound as if she was joking.

"Nothing," snapped her sister. "It's just—it's mine."

"All right."

"All right."

"All *right*!" said Marie, holding her hands up in surrender.

"Go to bed on time," Héloise muttered. "I'll let Adrien know I won't be home." And she flew out the door.

Marie could have minded her own business. But then what kind of little sister would she be?

She waited until she had the right moment. It was a Sunday, when the Germans were doing their obnoxious march down the Champs. Their loud boots, their straight arms, their hideous green uniforms. They made Marie want to spit.

Héloise said she was going for a walk in the Jardin de Luxembourg after Mass.

"A walk?" asked Marie. "Again? It's freezing." They needed to wear their shawls and thickest sweaters to bed every night. Why on earth would Héloise want to spend more time outside than necessary? She seemed to always be going on long strolls these days.

"It's hardly colder out here than it is in the apartment. Besides, I feel cooped up," said Héloise. Well, *that* Marie understood. The apartment was so small that it could seem stifling at times.

"I'll walk Marie home before work," said Adrien.

"You're working today?" asked Héloise with surprise.

"There's so few of us left to wait tables. I'm lucky to have a job at all, not that more money gets me any more rations."

"I don't need anyone to walk me home," protested Marie. "You two go ahead. It's only a few blocks."

Adrien glanced up the street, hesitating, but to Marie's surprise, Héloise shrugged.

"If she says she's fine, she's fine," Héloise told him.

Marie turned left as if she was about to go home, trying to ignore the biting wind. But as soon as her sister and almost-brother were out of sight, she turned and peeked around the church. Adrien had turned the corner toward Café Fleur-de-Lis. But Héloise had continued straight. Cautiously, Marie began to follow her.

Her sister didn't make it easy. The sidewalks felt emptier than usual, and Marie felt as if she were wearing a giant sign that read CAUTION: ATTEMPTING TO BE SNEAKY. Héloise was constantly glancing behind her, eyes looking around warily while Marie hid behind a garbage can or tucked herself into a corner. If Héloise was trying not to look suspicious, she was failing miserably. At one point, Héloise looked over her shoulder so suddenly that Marie had to leap into an alley, where she crashed into a boy on his bicycle. She had to stop, apologize, and quickly help him collect all the papers that fell from his knapsack.

Héloise was going more quickly now, turning a sharp right on a crowded street. Marie was trotting after her, when suddenly—

"Halt."

A hand on her shoulder.

Marie froze, feeling her blood turn quickly to ice. This wasn't the first time she'd been stopped by a German. She'd been living in occupied Paris, this horrible sea of secrets and rations and boots, for three and a half years. But it was the first time she'd been stopped when she was completely alone, and it was definitely the first time she'd been stopped while chasing down her sister who might or might not be reading a secret Resistance newspaper.

Marie looked at the soldier carefully.

"Bonjour," she said quietly.

He looked young—not much older than Adrien. He had a thick mustache with a few lingering crumbs in it. He smiled, and small creases appeared around his eyes.

"Where are you off to in such a hurry?" he asked, curiosity dripping from his heavily accented French.

"I—" Her heart leapt into her throat. Where, where? "I was just . . ."

"Marie!" Jeanne bounded up to the two of them, a giant smile on her face. Jeanne! Marie exhaled. There was something about Jeanne that always made Marie feel safe, even while standing in front of a German. Jeanne threw her arm around her. "Wandering off to the bookshop again, I suppose? I told you to go straight home after Mass. It's too chilly out for exploring!"

The soldier glanced at Jeanne. "Your sister?"

"Oui, of course," said Jeanne easily. "Always with her nose in a book. She finished her latest in only a day. But of course it's much too cold out here—and you could slip on the ice with that running! The books aren't going anywhere, silly girl."

Something about Jeanne's easy confidence gave it to Marie as well. She smiled her best little-girl smile, for once trying to look younger than she was.

"But I've got my pocket money from watching Madame Brassard's little ones," Marie complained. "I need to find out what happens next with the detective!"

Jeanne grinned down at her, patting her shoulder. "Then we shall go together quickly before heading home for lunch. Good day, sir."

As they turned to walk away, the soldier put out a hand. "Wait."

They turned back. Jeanne still seemed easy, breezy, as joyful as the Paris sun on a spring morning. Marie could do the same, surely.

But the German simply looked at her, smiling a bit sadly.

"You look so much like my little sister," he said. "Her name is Gisela."

Jeanne and Marie simply stood there, looking at him.

"She must be very proud," Marie forced out, "to have a brother doing his duty for his country." The words rotted like mold in her mouth.

At that, the soldier laughed, a harsh sound. "If only more of you French saw it that way. Anyway. Carry on, and slow down."

He turned and stalked away, a French family a few meters away parting slightly to let him through.

Jeanne, still smiling, slid her arm through Marie's and yanked her down the street cheerfully, as if the German had been an old friend she'd had the pleasure of chatting with.

"Where are we going?" Marie asked in a hushed voice.

"Why, to the bookshop, of course!" said Jeanne brightly. Their ruse was not up yet.

Almost the minute they got into the small, dusty bookshop, Jeanne dropped her hand.

"Good job," she said quietly, glancing around the shop.

"Thank you for helping me."

Jeanne chuckled, grabbing a faded purple book off the shelf and flipping through it casually. "Let's just say I've had plenty of practice. Where *were* you off to in such a hurry?"

Marie bit her lip. Part of her desperately wanted to tell Jeanne. After all, she was one of her sister's best friends. And Jeanne always spoke so distastefully of the Nazis. Surely she'd understand?

On the other hand, it was hard to know who to trust. She thought of Adrien's words: Stay in your rabbit hutch. Keep your head down.

And yet... what kind of life was that? Marie's world had gotten so small without Papa, without Sarah. It was dull lessons and Clarisse's blathering; it was cold hands and chattering teeth and lining up at the butcher for a tiny sliver of meat. She longed to tell someone, at least one person, what she was really, truly, thinking. Just this once.

"I was following Héloise," she admitted, so quietly that she was practically whispering. "I found... something... in her bag."

Jeanne raised an eyebrow. Like always, she looked perfectly poised—every hair in place, her scarf tied just so. Her lips were bright red—where on earth had she been able to find lipstick? Héloise hadn't had any in years. "What kind of something?"

Marie glanced around, but there was nobody in the store except for the ancient clerk. Monsieur LeClare was hard of hearing, and besides, she'd heard him mutter prayers every Sunday at Mass for the Germans to finally leave.

"A newspaper. A *Resistance* newspaper. Having

one—it's illegal. But it made me think she was up to something. She's so rarely been home lately. And my sister . . . she keeps things close. Doesn't share much. She could be bringing down the entire German army and I'd have no idea," admitted Marie.

"Hmm," mused Jeanne. "A newspaper. Not such a big deal, is it?"

"We saw a woman with that same newsletter get whipped with a pistol in the street a couple of weeks ago," bit out Marie. "Not a big deal to us, maybe. But a very big deal to the Nazis."

Jeanne nodded. "True. So, you were following to see if she was going to get another?"

"Or if she was . . . I don't know. Meeting someone. Making plans. It sounds ridiculous," Marie admitted.

"Not so ridiculous," said Jeanne in a hushed voice. "Perhaps a bit imaginative. Lots of people read things about the Resistance. That doesn't mean they're fighting for De Gaulle." De Gaulle was appalled that Marshal Pétain had given up France so easily, and he believed that even the free areas of France were under Nazi control.

"Maybe so," said Marie.

Jeanne picked up another book, and Marie's heart dropped. *Le Petit Lapin Rose.* Her father's book. In a moment, a thousand images flashed before her eyes: Papa, sketching. Papa, daydreaming. Papa, spinning tales of rabbits and birds and mice, keeping worry and woe at bay.

If only he were here. What would he tell her to do? What would he say about Héloise?

"Stay in our rabbit hutches, yes?" said Jeanne, flipping through the book as if she'd read Marie's mind. "Stay safe."

Marie nodded. Jeanne and Adrien were right. She should keep her head down. After all, Papa had trusted the marshal. Perhaps she should too.

But that night, when both sisters had made it back home and Héloise was fast asleep, Marie lay in bed and waited for her sister's telltale snoring. Héloise may have been slick on the streets of Paris, but she was about as subtle as a German Mercedes while she slept. Marie crept out into the kitchen, carefully stepping over the creakiest floorboards, and found her sister's bag hung on a chair. She opened the flap, being sure not to move things around too much.

There it was—a new copy of *Défense de la France*.

And now too—a note stuck to it with a paper clip.

2217 Rue de Augustine.

An address.
What was Héloise up to?

And what was on Rue de Augustine?

The snoring stopped, and somehow the silence was even louder. Marie shut the bag as quickly as she could.

"Marie?" Héloise called out sleepily. "Is that you?"

"Just fetching some water," she called back.

When did she become this person—a girl who lied to her sister? Not the small fibs of their childhood; not bickering over a stolen sweater or a snatched hair bow. Real lies with sturdy shapes, rising out of her heart like steam.

Perhaps the war had turned them all into people they hadn't been before. She pulled her shawl more tightly around her, willing herself to believe that her shivers came from the sharp winter air and nothing more.

October, present day

PENNY HURRIED DOWN the street, pulling her North Face jacket more tightly around her and shivering from the sharp autumn air. She was in a hurry to meet her mom at the Musée de l'Orangerie. She had no idea why her mom had texted her to meet her there, or why a museum would be named after oranges, but she was getting sick of sitting in her apartment doing schoolwork with the Hogwarts Library ASMR full-blast in her AirPods.

Well, *kind of* doing schoolwork. Homeschooling was different than she was used to, but she surprisingly liked it. Dad simply gave her a little list each morning of what she had to get done, and she did it. He helped when she needed him to, which hadn't been often.

Today she'd rushed through her math workbook and done a little reading for religion. The YouTube video on ecosystems she was supposed to watch for science was so boring she'd almost fallen asleep. Did walking briskly to an art museum count as gym class?

Really, she'd spent most of the morning doing small chunks of schoolwork between thinking about the letter she'd found. That was sufficient for history class, right? She'd googled Marie Bonnet a million times, but still hadn't found a single thing.

There was, of course, a practical reason she wanted to find out who the painting belonged to. It was probably worth a fortune. Not a "fortune," like Mrs. Woodward had paid her to watch her twins on Saturday afternoons back in Fernridge Falls, but a *real* fortune. The article Mom had showed her priced it at five *million* dollars. Five million dollars! If Penny solved the mystery and located the owner—well. Who's to say they wouldn't be so grateful that they gave her a reward? Who's to say Mom even *had* to work at her fancy art historian job anymore? Who's to say they couldn't get right back on an airplane to America?

But it was more than that too. Larger and more layered. It was because, for some reason, when Penny looked at that painting, she felt something stirring inside her. Some kind of recognition, as if maybe she'd seen it before, a really long time ago. Something that made her pause and look longer than she needed to.

That was what the best art did, Mrs. Marley had always told her. Made you pause and look, even when you had somewhere else to be.

Penny had never been able to do that with her art, no matter how hard she tried.

Mom was waiting on a bench outside the museum, sipping from a paper cup.

"There you are," Mom said. "Did you know most places in Paris don't do to-go coffee? I had to find a Starbucks." Oh, she knew.

"What are we doing here?" asked Penny, shivering.

"Come on. Let's go inside." They went through security, walking quickly through a metal detector and putting their phones in little containers to be scanned like they were at an airport. Even though it was a random Tuesday morning, the museum was packed, with long lines out the door and groups huddled in every corner, looking over museum maps and chattering in Japanese and Polish and Spanish. Penny saw a sign that explained that the museum was called the Orangerie because it used to store citrus trees during the winter.

"Do you know where we are?" Mom asked conspiratorially, tossing her empty cup into a garbage can.

"Um . . ." Penny glanced around. "An art museum."

"An art museum. An art museum, she says!" Mom

wiggled her eyebrows. Clearly, she was pleased with herself. "Penelope Rose Marks, we are at one of the greatest art museums in the world. Do you know *why*?"

"Why?" asked Penny flatly, trying to keep every inch of excitement out of her voice. Keeping up her role as family grump was getting a little exhausting.

"Because it," Mom said, "has the Water Lilies."

Okay, *that* made Penny's jaw drop. "*The* Water Lilies? As in—"

"As in, Claude Monet! As in, the greatest impressionist of all time! As in, one of the most beautiful paintings to ever exist is on the other side of that wall!"

Just the thought of being so close to some of her favorite paintings made Penny shiver, and this time, it wasn't from the bitter chill. There, right *there*—she was close to some of the greatest art ever painted.

Well, her and a thousand other tourists.

Penny turned to go in, but Mom grabbed her shoulder. "Wait. Remember, we have to be quiet."

It was indeed silent in the large, oval-shaped room, except for a few whispers of "Take my picture" and "Where's the bathroom?" Stretched alongside one long wall wasn't just *any* water lily painting: it was her favorite, *The Water Lilies—The Clouds*. It had deeper, richer colors than the other canvases, and it made Penny want to fall into the pond and live inside Monet's world. She could see his brushstrokes—she was close enough to touch them, although she was sure it would set off a million alarms.

She stood and stared at the painting. Again, that feeling swelled up in her: the feeling of wanting to simply *look* at something, for a very, very long time. There weren't words she could use to describe it. There wasn't a way to explain. She felt a core of *awe* bubble up in her body. There was a piece of Claude Monet, and a piece of Penny Marks, and those pieces were clashing and colliding and swirling around the room, spreading light wherever they landed. She almost got dizzy with the weight of it.

She took it all in for a while before Mom came over and gently patted her shoulder.

As they stepped back out into the October sunshine, Penny blinked up at the sky, as if she'd just emerged from a dark, cold tunnel.

"Wow," she said. She couldn't pretend to not be moved. There were times Penny wished she could hate art, wished she could be as moved by news stories as Erin and Rosalie were. "How much do those *cost*?" Rosalie would have asked. "They could probably feed an entire village in a third-world country." No, "developing nation." You didn't say "third-world country" anymore, and Rosalie always knew stuff like that.

But as much as Penny wished she could think it was a stupid waste of time, she was the kind of person who was moved by paintings of water lilies. She just was.

"I know," Mom said, giddy. "I *knew* you'd love them."

"Why didn't we come sooner?"

"Well, there's a thousand and one art museums in Paris, Pen. We have to savor them. Can't just *rush* these things." Rushing art was one of Mom's biggest pet peeves. Mrs. Marley's too. Whether you were creating or admiring, they both believed you should linger.

Mrs. Marley had loved Monet's water lilies. Penny wondered if she'd ever seen them in person. She suddenly had an urge to email her, but she didn't want to be obnoxious. Who wanted to hear from a former student who'd yelled at you? From a kid that didn't stand up for you, that let you be tossed out of the school like a crumpled old Culver's bag? There'd been a meeting about axing the art program. All these people had gone and spoken out. Mom had been on the news. But Penny had stayed home. She'd been so embarrassed about quitting painting that she hadn't even said goodbye on Mrs. Marley's last day.

She and her mom walked home arm in arm.

"Isn't it funny," mused Mom, "that we're the only creatures that actually seek out beautiful things? Dogs don't go outside just to watch the sunset. Birds don't stop and admire lovely gardens. It's just us humans who admire something beautiful just for being beautiful."

Penny nodded. "Well, some people don't like the water lilies. Mrs. Marley showed me an essay last year by a guy who said the impressionists were lazy and that's why they don't have firm lines."

"What do you think she was trying to teach you?" Mom asked.

"That art is subjective," Penny said. "That different things might be beautiful to different people."

"Exactly. We all have our different tastes and preferences. We all come from different cultures too, and bring our own histories. The important thing is that we never stop seeking the beautiful, right? That's what keeps us *human*."

"Well," said Penny. "Maybe."

"But?"

"But if you don't like the water lilies, you need to get your eyes checked."

Mom laughed, pulling Penny in tighter and throwing her arm around her shoulder. "I don't disagree with you there, kid."

Suddenly, a siren blared in Penny's ear as a police car raced down the street. Then another.

"Yikes," Mom said. "Must have been an accident."

Another came by a moment later. People started to walk more quickly down the sidewalk, dipping around them. Everyone seemed like they were in even more of a hurry than usual. Mom and Penny ducked under a pharmacy awning for a second, Mom pulling out her phone and glancing at it to text Dad that they were on their way home. Her eyes went from *Huh?* to *Oh!* to . . . something like *fear*.

"Come on," Mom said, turning a corner and pulling Penny behind her. "Let's hurry."

"What's going on?" asked Penny.

"I'll tell you back at the apartment. I promise. Focus on walking quickly, please."

More people were hurrying—everyone looking at their phones. Some people shouting in French. Another cop car, and another twisty street—why did Paris have so many winding streets? Why wasn't anything *straight*? The whole city was like one big impressionist painting—splashes of color and smears of motion.

Penny was relieved when they began to pass familiar things that were close to their apartment—the statue of Louis XIV in the Place des Victoires, and the Théâtre du Palais-Royal. It was wild how quickly such massive, stunning sights had become commonplace to her. Finally they were at the small door of their apartment building on the corner. Mom quickly pounded the code into their keypad and hurried Penny in, shutting the building door tight behind her.

"*Penny!* And Pippa! Oh my gosh." There was Dad, waiting anxiously at their front door. He practically yanked them inside and hugged them, tight. Her brothers were sitting in front of the TV, their faces white.

The news was on—American news, actually; CNN. Dad must have hooked it up with his phone somehow. A serious-looking woman was talking about Paris.

"Just thirty minutes ago, a man yielding a knife attacked three British tourists in the heart of Paris, standing on the Pont Royal. Our Paris correspondent, Brian Lee, is on the ground. Brian?"

"Amanda, Paris police apprehended the man that they say brutally attacked three tourists from London. A mother and two daughters were—"

Mom grabbed the remote and turned the TV off.

"Hey!" both boys and Dad protested.

"Max, if you want to watch the news, you can do it on your iPad in our room. Boys, you have schoolwork to do."

"But Mom, the guy was *right here*," said Mason.

"Everyone on Reddit is saying it's a terrorist attack," said Matthew, glancing down at his phone.

"Reddit? What are you doing on Reddit? You're not supposed to be on Reddit."

"Mom, look at a calendar. Nobody watches CNN anymore."

"Well, that includes you. Go find something to do that isn't doom-scrolling, please," Mom said, exasperated. Penny watched as Dad ducked into their room. His face was intense, staring at his iPad screen.

Everyone dispersed, but Penny just stared at the TV. The beauty of the water lilies was long forgotten, even though the paintings were still there, pinned to the walls in the dark museum. The lights were surely off by now. She couldn't even remember what they'd looked like.

January 1944

MARIE COULDN'T EVEN remember what the market had looked like before the Germans came. She and Clarisse wandered through the empty street, pretending the stalls were full of croissants and chicken and bread. Anything, anything to eat. They were freezing, but they were freezing inside just as badly, and at least out here they could feel the sun was poking through the clouds. At the beginning of the war, the stalls had still been bursting with flowers. Hitler had demanded that Paris stay full of flowers. They would keep Paris beautiful, he'd insisted, honoring it as the City of Light. But now the flower stalls were closed. Maman would be horrified. She thought flowers brought necessary beauty to every room.

Clarisse was blathering again, barely stopping to

take a breath, and it drove Marie crazy. Her father this, her father that. According to Clarisse, her father was going to save all of France. "Well, he'd better hurry up with it," Marie wanted to snap. Again, she missed the days before the war, when Sarah had rounded out their friendship. Without her there, everything felt off-kilter. A tricycle with a wheel missing. One day she'd be back, and perhaps then Clarisse wouldn't seem quite so obnoxious.

But she knew that was being naive. Sarah might never come back. It gave her a creeping feeling of horror to think of it, like someone had taken a knife and was scraping out her insides. Some people even seemed pleased that all the Jews had disappeared—she'd heard Madame Brassard in the apartment staircase the other day, talking loudly with her sister about the "Jewish filth" the city had been cleaned of. And what had Marie done? Nothing. She'd been as cowardly as a little pink rabbit. Her cheeks burned with shame at the memory.

Finally Clarisse headed home, her threadbare scarf pulled tight around her neck. Marie wanted to wander still; she didn't feel like going back to the lonely apartment and sitting there in silence. Even Clarisse's chattering would be preferable to the dead quiet. Héloise was at the Ritz so often these days, making beds for Germans and running errands for Germans and serving coffee to Germans.

And that address—it burned in her pocket.

Two-two-one-seven Rue de Augustine.

She wandered down the Rue de Rivoli by herself, past pigeons perched on wrought-iron gates and mothers hurrying by, clutching the hands of their children. She passed the Louvre, Paris's beloved art museum. The Place Vendôme, with its giant Nazi flags facing the square. It made her ill to see the Ritz and think of her sister inside.

She turned sharply down a side road, letting herself meander with no real destination in mind. She knew she would be in trouble if stopped. She wasn't supposed to be just wandering the streets, and her fingers were starting to numb. But something kept her walking down the cobbled streets, imagining a time when she could do so without the sound of les Boches' boots marching in her ears.

Sometimes it made Marie ache, to think of a time when the Germans had left. Clarisse loved to fantasize about such a thing—when they could go back to the cinema, when all the men would come home, when De Gaulle would lead them all to victory.

But what if that never happened? What if every

Christmas was the same as the last—no bûche de Noël, no caroling at midnight Mass, no Papa to tell her old stories of Père Noël that she was much too old to believe? What if every spring, the flower stalls stayed as empty as ever? What if every summer was spent sweating through mandatory parades down the Champs Élysées? What if every winter was spent cold, *so* cold, a biting cold that snuck through her fingers and spat out frost? What if she never saw Sarah or Papa again? What if this was the rest of her life in Paris?

Suddenly she heard a whistle. It was soft and low and familiar. Maman had sung it to her a thousand times.

"La Marseillaise," the national anthem of France.

She glanced across the street and saw a boy about her age, walking with his hands stuffed deep in his pockets. His head down, he was whistling the song with all of the power his lungs held.

Arise, children of the Fatherland.
Our day of glory has arrived.

He turned the corner, disappearing into a shadowy street. Marie closed her eyes. She couldn't stop hoping for Paris's day of glory. She couldn't let her heart turn rotten with despair. What good would that do anyone? Would it make the future any less painful?

She paused to look around. Somehow she'd gotten a bit lost, caught up in the twists and turns of the Parisian streets. She could just see the statue of Apollo hoisting his lyre above the Palais Garnier. She would make her way to the opera house and find her way home from there.

But as she turned down yet another side road, she noticed the name of the street.

Rue de Augustine.

Héloise. That address.

Perhaps Paris would stay under siege forever, but Héloise was doing something to stop the Germans. Marie knew it; she knew it the way sisters simply *know* things about each other. She knew it the way she could tell by Héloise's footsteps what kind of mood she was in, and the way she knew her sister would always pause to look at the pigeons in the Jardin de Luxembourg and choose a chocolate croissant over an almond one. She *knew* her sister, and she knew she was up to something. Now Marie could finally discover what.

She picked up her pace, practically trotting down the street; 2207, 2209—

"Ow!"

Marie fell to the ground, hard, her shoes flying out from underneath her as she landed on her rear end. She winced in pain, rubbing the shoulder that had slammed into someone in a hurry.

"Marie! I'm so sorry!" A hand reached down to help her up. It was Jeanne, in a bright blue beret, her eyes sparkling. "You poor thing."

"I'm all right," Marie insisted. Her heart gladdened to see that it was Jeanne, who could cheer her up on the very worst days. Jeanne was always so full of hope, she made Marie think anything was possible. Anything at all.

"You're in a hurry," said Jeanne with a grin. "Again. Where are you off to at such a speed, hmm?"

Marie shrugged. "Honestly, I don't know. I was just on a walk."

"In this cold?"

"It's just as cold indoors," Marie reminded her.

"True," Jeanne admitted, rubbing her own hands on her arms. "But where were you walking to?"

Marie opened her mouth. Closed it. Opened it again. She could trust Jeanne. She knew she could.

"It's Héloise," she whispered. "She had an address for this street written on a piece of paper, and I just—I think she's up to something. I think she's fighting against les Boches somehow. I don't know how. I don't have proof. But I—"

Jeanne simply smiled, her bright red lips curling up gently.

"What happened to your little rabbit hutch?" she asked Marie.

Marie looked to her feet. "Jeanne d'Arc didn't stay in her hutch, and neither will I."

They stood there together, a moment of silence. Jeanne seemed to be considering something. An extra strong gust of wind blew down the street, making Jeanne reach up to grip her beret to her head.

"Well," she said quietly, "perhaps we should finish this conversation indoors. Come with me."

With her other hand, she reached forward and grabbed Marie's, sliding their fingers together. They looked like two sisters on a simple walk down an empty Parisian block, on their way to queue up at a bakery that surely wouldn't have any bread.

They stopped in front of a shabby-looking building; 2217 looked as if it had seen better days. There was rust on the iron handrail, and chunks of concrete had chipped away from the steps. The window box of flowers hadn't been tended all winter; there was simply a brown-and-yellow clump of thorny weeds hanging from it. It looked like any other Parisian apartment, but Jeanne walked up with complete confidence, opening the door as if she owned the place.

"Jacques!" she called out. "It's me. I have your shoes from the cobbler, all mended just right."

Marie, confused, followed Jeanne up the narrow staircase, past windows so small their faces could barely poke out. The two girls arrived at the top floor, and Jeanne happily trotted through another door, bringing Marie along with her.

The room was untidy, but still somehow organized Two boys about Adrien's age stood near the window, smoking a single cigarette between them, and another woman, a bit older than Jeanne, slept in a dark blue flowered chair in the corner. A small round table sat in the middle of it, covered with various stacks of papers. Sitting at the table was a young woman. She turned, her braid flying over her shoulder, and when her eyes met Marie's, they both widened.

It was Héloise.

"Welcome," said Jeanne calmly, "to the Rue de Augustine."

Héloise jumped up, almost knocking over the cup of water she'd been drinking. "Marie, what on earth are you doing here?" Her eyes flashed through a thousand emotions—she was scared, she was angry, she was concerned, she was bewildered.

"Someone should be a bit more careful, Héloïse," said Jeanne, tut-tutting with her tongue. She tossed the bag of shoes she'd been holding onto the table and flopped herself down into a chair. "You left the address written on a piece of paper in your bag? How many times have I told you—"

"You went through my *bag*?" said Héloïse to Marie, her voice thick with accusation.

"Wait. Just wait a minute." Marie glanced around. The other three people in the room hadn't even acknowledged her. "Where *are* we? What is this?"

"You shouldn't have gone through my things. You're always doing that. Last summer, she stole one of my scarves and spilled tea all over it—"

"I barely dripped on it, and you threw a fit—"

"It was from *Maman*—"

"For heaven's sake, you two. Cut it out." Jeanne slammed her palm down on the table so loud that the Bonnet sisters jumped. "This isn't a scarf, Héloïse! It's vital information to the Resistance, and you left it lying about like a spare pencil."

"I'm sorry," she muttered, her cheeks rosy from embarrassment. "I didn't mean—"

"The Resistance?" said Marie. "Is this . . . is this, like, a meeting place?"

"Your sister has been incredibly helpful to us," said Jeanne calmly.

"Us?" Small things clicked together in Marie's mind: her sister and Jeanne's frequent meetings, Jeanne's red-and-blue apparel, the *Défense de la France* tucked into Héloïse's bag. "You . . . you're working together?"

"'Working together' is a strong phrase," said Héloïse. "I just—there are so many Germans at the hotel, Marie. They're careless. One of the busboys, he speaks German. He tells me what they say, I tell Jeanne . . . that's all. I'm more of an eavesdropper than anything else."

One of the boys chortled in the corner, and Marie glanced over.

"She's more than an eavesdropper," the boy said. "She's the only reason we knew which line the new train of German supplies was coming in on. Your sister fights for the liberation of France, and she does a great job doing it."

Héloïse blushed again.

"But . . . but you said we should stay safe in our rabbit hutches," Marie said to Jeanne accusatorily. "You said I was imagining things!"

"I can't go around telling every person in Paris the work we do," said Jeanne. Marie bristled. That was all she was to Jeanne? Just another *person in Paris?* "It's dangerous. You never know who will rat you out. I've lost many friends, Marie. I don't intend to lose the girls who've become like sisters to me."

More than just another person, then. A sister. Marie could barely let her heart warm at the sentiment before the boy burst in again.

"Jeanne, stay safe in a rabbit hutch?" he asked. "She's the bravest broad in all of France."

Jeanne laughed, and even Héloise cracked a small grin.

"That's Jacques, and Luc," Héloise said, nodding toward them. "They . . . help too. And—"

"And Pierre, who will be furious you didn't run the girl by him first," Luc butted in. He was talking to Jeanne only. "What are you thinking, just bringing a child up here?"

"I would trust Marie with my life," said Jeanne. "And Pierre, in case you've forgotten, answers to *me*. Not the other way around."

Luc rolled his eyes, putting out the final smudge of cigarette in an ashtray. "Writing down the address *was* foolish."

"I said I was sorry," snapped Héloise.

"But—since *when*?" Marie burst out.

"Only the past year or so," Héloise confessed, her

tone turning more timid. "Don't be angry with me, Marie. Jeanne told me I couldn't tell a soul. It *is* dangerous, like she said. The wrong piece of information in someone's mind, and before you know it . . . we've seen it, haven't we?"

They had. All of Paris had. The Resistance workers yanked away by police; the innocent children torn from their mothers. The woman with the newspaper, as they walked home from church. Marie's skin crawled. What if something like that happened to Héloise? What if—

"And after Sarah . . ." Héloise shut her eyes, and Marie's heart dropped. Sarah, with her musical laugh and endless stories. Her friend. "Oh, Marie . . . you were so upset, when she left. Didn't *leave*. Was taken. I couldn't stop thinking about her. She was always so kind to you. I had to do something. I met Jeanne, and when she found out where I worked, she said it could be useful."

"And it has been," said Jeanne quietly. "You've helped Sarah from afar, even though it doesn't feel like it."

"I never even told Papa what I was up to," Héloise said. "And now he's gone, and I couldn't do a single thing to stop it."

"Does Adrien know?" asked Marie. She had no idea what made her think of him, but she remembered him holding her tight in the apartment after they'd seen the woman get caught with the newspaper. She had a feeling she knew the answer.

Héloïse snorted. "No. And we need to keep it that way."

"We've never kept a secret from Adrien in our entire lives."

"Adrien wants to . . . how did you say it? Stay safe in his rabbit hutch. Like Papa's story." Héloïse shook her head bitterly. "He wants to just put his chin down and get through the war. Get through it, like it's the flu and enough water and fresh air will clean it up. He doesn't realize that we need to *do* something. And his job, at the café! He'd be so helpful."

"Have you even asked him?" said Marie.

"No. I don't want him to know that I'm . . . helping. Passing secrets. Eavesdropping. Whatever you want to call it. He doesn't need to know. I've heard him rant about Resistance workers plenty, almost as much as he complains about the Germans. He thinks they're taking unnecessary risks, causing trouble. He'd be furious with me, and . . . I don't want that."

A *whoosh* of anger flew through Marie like the wind, in and out just as fast. She wished Adrien would be as brave as her sister. She also hated the idea of him lined up against a wall by Germans. She wanted to keep him safe. But she wanted Sarah safe too. She wanted so many things, and everything seemed to be in conflict, clashing and colliding into one another. Who's *want* was more important? Who deserved what they wanted the most?

"I *am* sorry about letting Marie find the address," Héloise said. "I didn't know someone would be digging through my bag."

"Ah, yes. Because all of our private things are so private these days," Jeanne teased her. "It's all right. It was an honest mistake. In fact, it may have been a blessing, hmm?"

"A blessing?" asked Héloise. She played with a loose button on her coat. It was barely hanging on by a thread.

Jeanne turned to look at Marie, her smile back in place.

Marie felt, in that moment, an odd sort of stirring. It was the kind you would see in a lake on a calm summer day, just before a storm burst out. Things that had seemed smooth and glimmering on the surface began to roll and rattle. Ripples of a pebble landing, and those ripples expanding, expanding, expanding.

"Marie," said Jeanne quietly, "can you keep a secret?"

October, present day

NO MATTER HOW hard she'd tried to keep the letter a secret, Penny should have known one of her stupid brothers would find out eventually.

After what had happened on the bridge, she wasn't allowed to explore Paris on her own. On the one hand, she got it. She didn't want to walk around these winding streets either, even with Siri telling her which way to turn. She didn't want to be alone on the cobblestones with people she didn't know. People who might have things in their bags—people who might have *knives* in their bags. No, Penny didn't want any of that at all. She preferred to stay safe and tucked in at their Parisian apartment, where just her family knew the key code and her mom's computer had a CATHOLICS FOR NONVIOLENCE sticker.

But on the other hand, it complicated her mission a bit. There's only so much you could do from a laptop.

The clues she had were those two names—*Marie Bonnet* and *Jeanne*. She'd googled Marie Bonnet over and over, the way you look in the fridge four times before resigning yourself to finding nothing but ketchup and old grapes. There wasn't anything there. Marie Bonnet didn't have an internet footprint.

Penny felt her determination slipping with each day. There was so much she didn't know, so much that felt impossible to figure out. Who was Héloise, and who was Jeanne, and who was Marie? Why was Marie leaving at that particular point, when the war wasn't over yet? And *how* did Delphine Ollier's painting get behind the wall? The more Penny read about Delphine Ollier, the more she knew this: Delphine hadn't created art just to stick it in a hiding place. She'd fought for recognition tooth and nail as a woman, climbing her way up the ladder with thousands of people trying to knock her off. She remembered a book Mom had once showed her: *Women Artists in All Ages and Countries*. Mrs. E.F. Ellet had written, way back in 1859, that women should mostly paint flowers and still lifes because "such occupations might be pursued in the strict seclusion of home." Imagine Delphine showing

Elizabeth Ellet *this*. She wasn't a woman who believed she had to stay strictly in her home, that was for sure.

Penny had a sinking feeling that it had something to do with the war. That people didn't hide beautiful things away unless they had a very, very good reason to. And 1944 . . . well. It wasn't just any year in Paris, that was for sure.

She *also* had a sinking feeling that once Mom learned she had the letter, she was going to be in more trouble than she'd ever been before.

But this mystery—Penny knew she could solve it. And then, once she did . . . Mom would be so grateful. And happy to be back in the US, where they belonged. Mom might *seem* like she was loving Paris, but she had to miss the same things Penny did, right? Their giant backyard, and American peanut butter? Their own language, spoken everywhere they went? They'd make Netflix documentaries about the famous found painting, and Mom and Penny could watch them from the comfort of their old living room.

"What are you reading?"

Penny slammed her laptop shut so hard, she worried she'd break it. "Matthew! Go away." She'd had a Wikipedia page pulled up—*Nazi plunder*. But it gave her the creeps to be reading it by herself. Mom was at the institute. Mason and Matthew had already finished their schoolwork for the day and had been off playing soccer at the park with Dad. She was almost glad her oldest brother was home now.

Matthew rolled his eyes. He'd been running around the soccer field at the park, and he had sweat dripping through his hair. Penny winced and leaned away.

"Go take a shower."

"Tell me what you were looking at."

"No. It's just a stupid thing for school."

"You shouldn't use Wikipedia for *school*," said Matthew. "Anybody can edit it. You know that, right? It's full of misinformation."

"You sound like the politicians on TV. *Fake news*."

"I mean, if they're talking about *Wikipedia*, they have a point," said Matthew. "Come on, just tell me. It looked interesting."

Penny opened her mouth to tell him to leave her alone, but stopped and considered her options.

On the one hand, Matthew was . . . Matthew. A brother. Enemy number one through three, depending on the day. Matthew thought kicking a ball into a net was his greatest lifetime achievement.

Plus . . . well. The skateboard. years ago, Mom and Dad had gotten Mason a skateboard for Christmas. He'd been begging for one all autumn. They'd even had it signed by a friend of a friend of a friend who'd been in the X Games; Penny couldn't remember who it was. Matthew had let it slip about five seconds after he'd seen it in the basement. Mom and Dad's Big Surprise was totally ruined, and they ended up just giving it to Mason early instead of making him wait. Matthew wasn't exactly known for keeping his mouth shut.

But . . . Matthew knew stuff about history.

Lots of stuff about history.

He could be useful in the mission. She didn't have to tell him the specifics, necessarily. She could use him for his brains and then drop him like a hot potato. A little evil genius-y, but hey. When you're the only girl in the family, sometimes you need to put on your mad scientist hat.

"Well," she said, "I'm doing a little research on . . . hidden things."

"Hidden things," said Matthew slowly. "What kind of hidden things?"

"Like, things that were hidden in 1944. Here in Paris."

"1944. The year Paris was liberated. So, things hidden from the Nazis?"

"Probably."

Matthew nodded, walking to the kitchen and opening the fridge. "Lots of things were hidden from the Nazis. They would take valuable things—sometimes things that were super expensive, but sometimes things that were just important to people. They'd send them back to Germany for the German people, or their own families. The higher-up guys would give their wives fancy jewelry they stole from Jewish people. It's sick."

Penny shuddered. That *was* sick. She thought of her most prized possessions—her drawing pencils, or the small Miraculous Medal bracelet from her nana. If those got stolen, she'd be heartbroken. She'd feel even worse if they wound up in the hands of someone truly evil.

Matthew took out the orange juice and indulged in a long swig straight from the carton.

"Gross," Penny complained, and he let out a long, loud belch. She lived with *animals*, honestly.

"What's this project for? History?" he asked.

"Yeah," she lied. "So if people hid something, it was probably so that the Germans wouldn't get it?"

"Exactly. It could have been worth a lot of money, or just had a lot of sentimental value to them. Germans stole *tons* of art, because Hitler wanted to make a huge art museum in Germany. He actually really liked art—he wanted to be an artist himself. He got denied by the Academy of Fine Arts in Vienna."

"What's that?"

"An art school. Kind of like the Sorbonne." That was

the ginormous university in Paris with an amazing art program. Mom had walked her around its campus only a few days after they'd moved, excitedly explaining its admissions process to Penny. As if Penny would ever get into a real art school like that.

"My project is about Marie Bonnet too," said Penny, trying to seem relaxed, as if she'd just said "George Washington" or "Harriet Tubman." Someone *everyone* knew about. It was a long shot, but maybe, just maybe—

"Who?" said Matthew, his nose wrinkled. Darn. Penny sighed. Her brother knew the names of tons of famous people from World War II. Marie Bonnet was probably a total nobody, just like her.

"She might have been in the Resistance," Penny explained, on the off chance that her discovery of multiple Adriens on that "French Resistance" Wikipedia page could maybe trigger something about Marie for Matthew. "But . . . you've never heard of her?"

"No," admitted her brother. "But honestly, it's not surprising. The French don't give enough credit to how many women and children were in the Resistance."

"Children?" Penny's eyebrows skyrocketed. "There were kids helping to get rid of the Germans?"

"Dude, *totally*." Matthew's eyes lit up, and he bounced on the balls of his feet. "Most of the men were sent to Germany to work in factories, or they were arrested. The Nazis were *afraid* of the men, you know? They thought the young men would lead an uprising. But the women and the kids could be so much sneakier, and they did a ton of damage. Under-the-radar type stuff. Kids could go most places, and they were small, so nobody suspected them. They could transmit messages, work radios. . . ."

So Marie Bonnet could have been a *kid*? Woah.

"Where did you hear of her? A book or something?" Matthew asked.

Penny was about to lie or tell him it was none of his business. Besides, his boy stink was really starting to get to her. She opened her mouth to tell him so, but then—

She stopped.

And she didn't know why.

She didn't know why, other than . . . ever since moving to Paris, she'd felt that creeping sense of aloneness. She had hardly anyone to talk to, besides her mother, who she was still mad at most of the time. That all-alone-in-the-universe feeling clung to her, and here was her brother. Not teasing her, or ranting about the Milwaukee Wave soccer team, or ganging up on her with Mason. But actually *talking* to her, and being interested in what she was interested in.

And it felt, in a weird way, kind of nice. Like something they could have a real conversation about that didn't involve soccer trophies.

Like he saw her as a person, instead of just a nuisance.

She took a deep breath. "I . . . found a letter she wrote. Okay? I found a letter she wrote, and I'm just trying to figure out who she was. That's all."

"A letter?" His eyes widened. "*Cool*. Can I see it?"

She narrowed her eyes. "The skateboard . . ."

He put a hand to his heart. "I solemnly swear to secrecy! And let me remind you, I was *thirteen* when I did that."

"I'm thirteen now! And I wouldn't blab!"

"C'mon, Pen. Please?"

No. "Sure." Who was she? Sharing secrets with her *brother*? But something made her reach down into her sketchbook, where she kept the letter neatly folded. She handed it to him, and he took it carefully.

"It's old," she warned him. "Don't smudge it."

"Oh my gosh," he muttered, looking over it. "This is . . . wow, Penny. This is really, really amazing. Where'd you *get* this?"

Well, she couldn't have him ruining her *whole* plan, could she? "The library. It was in a book."

"Woah. Okay, so first things first—you googled her. Obviously."

"I did," she said. "And it came up with a few LinkedIn profiles and some stuff in French. Not super helpful."

"Didn't you use Google Translate?"

"Yeah, but none of it was her. I couldn't find anything, I'm telling you."

"And Jeanne—no last name. What about Héloise?"

"She doesn't have a last name either."

"Right, but they're leaving *together*, it sounds like," Matthew said slowly. "So . . . sisters, probably? Maybe?"

Sisters—obviously! *We* need to leave, *we* got papers . . . why hadn't she thought of that? Matthew whipped out his phone and plopped down on the couch. Penny scooted next to him, then wrinkled her nose. "You *seriously* need a shower."

"And you *seriously* need my help. Did you ask Mom? She probably has access to some databases at work—"

"No," said Penny quickly. "It's—it's *my* school thing. I want to do it without Mom."

"Whatever. Your deal. Okay, Héloise Bonnet . . . wow."

Penny's heart dropped—twenty-six million results. An indie singer, a poet, half a dozen TikTok accounts. To her surprise, Matthew went back to the search bar— *Héloise Bonnet obituary*.

"Obituary?" said Penny. "We have no idea if she's dead."

"But 1944 was a long time ago," he pointed out. "And she doesn't sound like a baby, necessarily. Just being realistic."

Still way too many results. But Matthew wasn't done.

Héloise Bonnet obituary + Marie + Paris.

"Bingo," he muttered. There it was, in the ... *Chicago Sun-Times*?

"America?" said Penny. "They lived in *Chicago*?"

"Now *that*," said Matthew, "is surprising."

"How come?"

"It was hard for people to emigrate to the US after the war," he said.

"We didn't want to let people in?"

"Well, sort of. It's more complicated than that. It was right after the biggest crisis the world had ever known. You had Nazis everywhere; you had to be careful about who you were letting into your country. But also ... a lot of politicians in the US didn't like Jews, or Catholics. And most refugees were Jewish or Catholic—especially if they were from France. So I'm not sure how they would have gotten to Chicago. But if it's the Héloise the letter is talking about, they did—and look."

Quickly, Penny and her brother read the obituary. Héloise Bonnet had died peacefully of leukemia in 2009, at the age of eighty-three. She was born in Paris, the daughter of prominent French children's writer Louis Bonnet and Celeste Bonnet. She left behind—

"A sister!" whispered Penny. "Marie Quinn! A sister who works for the Chicago public school system!"

Matthew reached over and grabbed Penny's laptop, his fingers flying across the keys. *Marie Quinn Chicago public schools.* There she was—an administrator, with a retirement party that was featured in the news. She'd won a fancy award for the district. Giant gold balloons and a cake from Costco.

"No contact information," said Penny. "How can we be sure it's her?"

"The photo," said Matthew. The caption read that she was standing with her daughter, Odette Shaffer, her son-in-law, Jake Shaffer, and her granddaughters, Gabrielle and Colette.

Odette Shaffer, Chicago. Not such a popular name. There she was—following in her mother's footsteps. The public school system. An English teacher, with a publicly listed email address.

"Boom shaka laka," said Matthew proudly.

Halloween in Paris was nothing like in America. There were no glittery orange pumpkins in store windows; no displays of witches and wizards in the parks. Hardly anybody trick-or-treated; they only had two or three children show up dressed up as farm animals, asking for "des bonbons ou un sor." ("Candy or a trick," Mom informed Penny. "Or . . . candy for my sister? I couldn't quite tell, so I just gave them a bunch of lollipops.")

Penny's history reading for school was about the Salem witch trials, but that was as celebratory as the day got. They'd tossed around the idea of going to an American restaurant, of which Paris had a few, but none of them really felt like going anywhere crowded so soon after the big attack.

Instead, the Marks family ended up having a supremely normal day, watching *It's the Great Pumpkin, Charlie Brown* in the evening after wolfing down pizza. Mom had gotten into sourdough baking and was desperately trying to score a loaf the way Paul Hollywood had done on *The Great British Baking Show* last week.

"Boo! You have to admit it," Dad said, bursting in the front door with a takeout box from the bakery next door. "Chocolate eclairs beat Halloween candy any day of the week." Dad was determined to make everyone in the Marks family think that Paris was the greatest place in the entire universe. He was like Paris's personal public relations representative, like the people celebrities hire to plant good stories about them in the press.

"Je voudrais ceci, s'il vous plaît," said Mason, reaching into the box before Dad even set it on the table.

"Your manners," said Dad, whacking his hand away, "are the scariest thing to me. Get a napkin, at least."

"I said please! Don't I get credit for that?"

"Wait!" said Mom, heaving her bright red Dutch oven out of the teeny-tiny French stove. "Look! I think it worked!"

Penny and Dad crowded around her.

"What do you think, Penny Lane?" Dad asked, seriously. "*Great British Baking Show* worthy?"

It wasn't perfect, but it was there—a vine and leaf pattern, carved into Mom's bread. And it smelled *delicious*.

"Yum," Penny said.

"Who cares what it looks like?" said Mason, a smear of chocolate frosting on his lips. "Can we eat some?"

Penny rolled his eyes. "We just had dinner. Do you ever—and yes, I do literally mean ever—stop eating?"

Mason considered this for a minute. "If I eat too close to the start of a game, I puke."

"*Here,*" Mom said, firmly interrupting, "is why it matters. You could just eat normal bread—a chunk of sourdough. And it would be good! It'd be fine. But isn't there something nice about eating with your eyes first? Isn't there a piece of you that wants to make something as mundane as bread a little more special, to remind you how special it *is* that we have food on the table and that we are all *together*?"

Dad swung his arm around Mom and gave her a quick, crisp kiss on the cheek. "You make everything more special."

Matthew and Mason pretended to gag, but Penny stared down at her mom's sourdough. The pattern wasn't perfect—the bread had split at the wrong point, and the lines weren't exactly even. The color, she knew Paul Hollywood would say, wasn't quite right; it needed a couple more minutes in the oven.

But there was something about a crowded Parisian living room with two lanky brothers, Snoopy on the television, a pumpkin candle burning, and a circle of bread with a delicate leaf pattern etched on top. No ambulances. No knives. Perfection felt pretty unattainable. But something she might even call close to beautiful was right there, within arm's reach.

January 1944

HERE IT WAS—HER chance to help Paris, just within arm's reach.

"No."

Héloise was always answering for her, as if she were a child. As if Marie didn't have a voice of her own, thoughts that were entirely hers. So much had been taken from her—her mother, her father, heat, food, her teachers, her friends. This choice would not be taken.

"This is *my* decision," Marie insisted. "Mine alone."

She sat at their rickety kitchen table, across from Jeanne and Héloise. The wind blew so cold outside that it rattled the windows, which were frosted thick with ice.

"Children are especially helpful," Jeanne said in a low voice. "They simply slip into the background. They are a part of Paris. They are flashes, blurs, innocent little bystanders...."

"I said no," repeated Héloise. "It's too dangerous. *I shouldn't even be—*"

"But you are," Jeanne reminded her.

Marie thought of the early days of the occupation. Papa, his hand firm on her shoulders. "They'll be gone soon," he'd assured her. "The old marshal has us."

The marshal had sold them out to les Boches in the time it took to whistle "La Marseillaise."

And now where was Papa? Gone. They didn't know where, but he wasn't coming back. Whispers floating down like rain about *the Americans, the Americans*, yet—where were they? Nobody was saving them.

Maman had taught her to love France, hadn't she? Red and blue ribbons braided in her hair, Bastille Day parties in the streets. La belle France. They couldn't just let it crumble under the boots of the Nazis. They couldn't let this happen to Maman's city. Penny was terrified—of both what could happen if she helped, and what could happen if she didn't.

"Héloise," she said, "it's up to me. I am going to help. I will be careful, just like you. And I will be brave, like Jeanne d'Arc."

Héloise slammed a hand on the table so hard that

the three of them jumped. "This isn't a story in a book, Marie!"

"Jeanne d'Arc isn't just a story, either!" Marie snapped back. "She was real. Jeanne is real. You are real. The people you work with, all trying to help, they're real. How will I live with myself, when Papa returns? Will I just say that I sat and did nothing?"

"You will say you stayed safe and sound, like your sister told you to."

Marie turned to Jeanne. "She can kick me out on the street if she likes. I don't care. I want to help. Please."

Knowing that Héloise was helping the Resistance had lit a flame in Marie that couldn't be put out. Her sister—her serious, studious sister, doing something as brave as fighting les Boches! Marie could not sit back while Héloise did everything for her. She was thirteen years old; plenty old enough to help in some way, surely. Marie was like Jeanne d'Arc—she didn't want to sit back and watch France burn.

She wasn't going to stay put in her rabbit hutch.

Jeanne glanced between the two sisters. She was trapped.

"Héloise," said Jeanne, "I think . . . we start small. Tiny things she couldn't possibly get into trouble for. Nothing like what you're doing. Small errands that won't even be noticed. And only after school."

"I can do something large," Marie insisted. "And any time of day! I want to do something that *really* helps."

"But—" Héloise started, but Jeanne cut her off.

"Marie, you're showing your age. Be helpful, not foolish. Not everyone needs to be Jeanne d'Arc. In fact, sometimes it's the smallest flickers of resistance that help us the most. Each and every spark counts. Because together . . ." She burst her hands open. "They create great fires!"

"Marie doesn't need to be a spark at all," Héloise bit out. "She needs to stay *safe*."

"Think of the other little girls who aren't in Paris any longer," Jeanne told her. "Think of the Jewish ones."

Marie had one last card to play. "Think of Sarah." Sarah, and her whole family. There one day and gone the next. They were Jewish, yes, but they were also *French*. As French as the Bonnet sisters.

With that, Héloise looked down at the table. Marie felt as if she was watching a glass shatter.

"Maman. Papa." Héloise looked at her sister, grief thick in her eyes. Her fingers picked at the burned piece of baguette in front of her. It had been all their ration cards had allowed them to get at the baker's. Héloise had stood in line for three hours for it. "Not you too. I can't."

Marie reached out and took her hand, folding their fingers together. Of course everything that had been taken from her had been taken from Héloise too. And even more. Héloise did not go to school; she did not have free time to read fairy tales. In that moment, Marie saw a thousand Héloises: the one who used to steal the larger slice of baguette, the one who skipped along the Jardin du Luxembourg, the one who whistled "Ave Maria" every Sunday, to applause from Maman and Papa. The one who had a permanent wrinkle of stress across her forehead, the one who went to work every single day and stood in line for hours to ensure that Marie had dinner to eat. It was like two different people sat before her, each fighting to be the victor.

"You won't," Marie said. "I promise."

Her first mission was simple.

A sack full of schoolbooks with papers tucked between their pages. Each piece of paper had a vertical line with two horizontal lines directly through it—the Cross of Lorraine. It was the sign of General Charles de Gaulle. Where Jeanne had even gotten spare paper, Marie had no idea. Paper was as hard to come by as food in Paris these days.

"It doesn't seem to be very important," said Marie, confused. She had thought she'd be smuggling secret messages or sneaking into German cars. Simply leaving sheets of paper on park benches didn't feel meaningful. How on earth would that bring Papa home? At the same time, it calmed her heart to know she wasn't immediately climbing through a Nazi's window or something.

Jeanne smiled at her. "Do you know what this cross means?"

"It's the sign of De Gaulle. The sign of Resistance."

"Exactly," said Jeanne. "Now, say you are a French mother who has been working and praying and waiting for the war to be over. You have very little food, for you and your four children. Your husband is a prisoner. Your heart is heavy. Your soul feels dry. You start to think . . . perhaps things really are over. Perhaps I should just give in to this horrid way of life. You get off the train, heading home after work. And what do you see on a bench in the station? This sheet of paper. This cross, reminding you that France is worth fighting for. Keeping your spirits up. Pushing you to live another day." Jeanne reached over and tucked one of Marie's blond ringlets behind her ear.

Marie thought of the day she'd seen the boy whistling "La Marseillaise"—how the simple tune had strengthened *her* spirits.

"Sometimes," Jeanne said softly, "the change starts in our hearts, yes? That can be where the biggest change takes place. The change in our hearts leads to a change in our actions. We strengthen hearts, we strengthen people. Remember what I said: Each and every spark matters. They're all little flickers breaking into the darkness. No matter how tiny they may seem."

Marie nodded. "I'll do it."

"It seems small because it is small. But les Boches are becoming more and more strict. Do you understand? Something as insignificant as this could lead to a horrible punishment. And just because you're a child doesn't mean they'll go easy. They will not."

Marie's heart flickered, but she smiled. "You're lucky Héloise isn't here. You said I was doing things I wouldn't possibly get into trouble for."

"Your sister loves you," said Jeanne, poking her in the chest. She pulled a ribbon from her satchel and tied her long brown hair up with ease. "You're lucky to have such a kind person looking out for you. But the truth is, these days, there's nothing you *couldn't* possibly get into trouble for. Les Boches are on the edge. They know the Americans are coming soon. It means we may not have to resist much longer, but it also means resisting is more dangerous than ever. Things that would have been ignored two years ago are things that could get you sent to jail now."

"Do you really think the Americans are coming?" asked Marie. She tried not to hear what Jeanne had just said—that she could get arrested. Go to jail. Never see her sister again. Marie had promised Héloise that her sister wouldn't lose her, and she would keep that promise.

Jeanne winked at her. "Let's just say I have very good sources, hmm?"

Marie tried to will some of Jeanne d'Arc's bravery into her heart as she walked through the train station. The trains were actually running, which was rarer and rarer these days. The schedules changed constantly for what seemed like no reason at all.

She wore her white ankle socks, to make her look even younger than thirteen. Her bag was heavy with the books Jeanne had loaded into it; all schoolbooks, nothing interesting to an officer. She approached a bench and glanced around as casually as she could. The station was bustling, which made her nervous that she would be seen. But also, she realized, this could be a good thing—there were so many people, who would even notice a little girl, leaving something behind on a bench?

She saw a small family, a mother with two daughters. Both girls had blond hair, just like her and

Héloise. The woman did not look like Maman, but she had the same kind eyes. She looked exhausted.

"I'm hungry, Maman," the shorter girl said.

Aren't we all, Marie thought.

"I know, my sweet. Let's pretend. Shall we have a delicious croissant?" The woman held up her hand to her mouth and acted as if she was biting it. The two girls giggled with delight.

Marie opened her bag and gently grabbed the stack of leaflets. Nobody watched as she placed them on the bench, refastened her bag, and kept walking, a bit more quickly.

Could it be that easy?

"Halt!"

Marie froze. Her heart beat so fast she could feel it in her knees. The fear that had been merely a seed bloomed in her belly and shot through her throat like acid. Stay calm, Jeanne had reminded her a thousand times. She'd said it was the most important thing. Stay calm, stay—

On the other side of the station, a German soldier had suddenly appeared. He almost looked like Adrien, with his dark hair and blue eyes. He grabbed the shoulder of a young blond man with a worn-out coat. He yelled something to another soldier in German, and the two grabbed the young man's shoulders, hauling him off.

"Stop!" the man yelled. "Stop! I didn't—"

The soldier reached into his backpack and pulled out a newspaper. "What is this? I saw you with this. You know what this is? You know reading these lies is illegal?" Marie recognized it—*Défense de la France*, the newspaper about the Resistance. The same one that the woman who had been pistol whipped in the streets had been caught with; the same one Héloise had tucked into her bag. She wondered if Héloise was the one who had given him the paper, or Jeanne, or another person she'd met at 2217 Rue de Augustine.

"It's not—"

"Quiet!" the first soldier barked. They turned down a corridor, and Marie put a hand to her mouth.

Nobody else even seemed to notice. Why should they? These things were commonplace now. People taken from their homes, from public places, for reasons you knew or didn't know. Maybe he was Resistance too. Maybe he was a Jew. Maybe the Germans were simply sending him to Germany to work, like Papa—he looked strong enough. It was like Jeanne had said. Things were much worse now than they had been a couple of years ago. More disappearances, more shouts of "Halt," more whispers in the wind of people taken and arrested. Paris was a shadow of itself. It was ashes and German pamphlets and a constant fear wrapping itself around your heart.

What if someone picked up one of her leaflets, and a German saw? What if it got them sent away from their family?

Jeanne was right. These may have been small things, but they were not simple. They were enormous choices with enormous consequences. She was not Jeanne d'Arc, charging across a battlefield, but she had won her own little war. She didn't dare glance back at the bench where she'd left the leaflets; instead she hurried back up the stairs and out of the station, holding her coat tightly around her. Her sister was waiting.

If Marie Bonnet was anything at all, she was Héloïse's sister, and she intended to keep her promises.

November, present day

IF PENELOPE ROSE Marks was anything at all, she was a world-class grumbler.

Honestly, she had an eye roll that could curl toes and make blood turn to ice. If she was in a bad mood, and wanted to make the rest of her family join in the pity party, she could do so with the snap of her fingers. She was an excellent heavy lifter of the weight of despair; she could find sadness and sorrow in the most cheerful of afternoons.

But even *she* was having a hard time being miserable in Paris in the autumn.

The golden leaves that seemed to dance on every corner, the little girls running around in embroidered sweater sets, the bakery windows with elegant displays of hot cross buns and seasonal fruit tarts—it all made her want to sit down and paint, if she was being honest.

She wanted to take a little slice of the sparkle and put it on a canvas. She wondered if she'd be able to capture the movement in the blur of sparrows flying south, or the perfect colors the sun made as it shimmered off of the glittering pavement, lightly dusted with frost.

And this too: As much as Penny had once shuddered at the idea of homeschooling, it was nice that their school day ended whenever they finished. She thought of Rosalie and Erin, who were probably still stuck in Mr. Buchheit's social studies class.

She was staring out the window, wondering which of her blue oil paints would best resemble the perfect Parisian sky, when Matthew burst out of his bedroom. "Okay, field trip. Anyone in? Dad said it was okay; I just texted him." Dad was getting some work done at a café up the street. He, the big homeschooling cheerleader, had discovered that working from home while all three Marks kids tried to do schoolwork gave him a headache. Mom was teaching a class.

But Penny had to get out of the apartment. She couldn't keep sitting there, refreshing her inbox and waiting for Odette Shaffer to reply to the email she'd sent last week. It had become an obsession, that refresh button and the dim blue glow of her laptop. She forced herself to look casual, but she jumped a little every time an email came through. Then she'd see that it was from one of her homeschool tutors, or from a clothing store, or from the prince of some far-off country asking for a loan.

"Anything to get me out of this documentary," said Mason, who was watching some video about different kinds of rock formations for his science class.

"Pen?" Matthew asked.

"Fine," she said. "But no soccer talk. I don't care who kicked what goal into what net in what country. Got it?"

"Got it," said Matthew.

"Who made you the boss?" asked Mason. But Matthew leaned over and whacked him upside the head as they all got their shoes on.

After a quick Metro ride, Penny found herself on a giant lawn, surrounded by important-looking buildings. There were groups of kids on real field trips everywhere. Matthew was asking a lady at the ticket counter something in French, and she was getting frustrated at his bad accent. She finally gave them what he was asking for—a map—and the three Markses headed toward one of the museums on the lawn.

"I've been wanting to go here for forever," said Matthew excitedly. "It's a museum all about the French Resistance effort."

"What?" Penny couldn't help herself. "So it might have something about—"

"Marie Bonnet?" Mason asked.

Penny turned to him. "How do *you* know about—"

"You think Matthew can keep secrets? The skateboard!"

Penny groaned.

"Come on, sister dear," said Mason, flinging his arm around her shoulders. "We're all invested, dude."

"Mason already knows half of Paris through his football club," Matthew pointed out. "I thought someone there might know something."

"Hey! I said no soccer talk!"

"That wasn't *talk*! That was *context*! I'm sorry," said Matthew.

"You swore!"

"Remember that old story about the scorpion stinging the frog?" It was one of Mom's favorite stories—a scorpion promises it won't sting a frog as it carries him across the lake. But then it does, even though it means they'll both drown. She was trying to prove the point that even if a scorpion swears it *won't* sting something, it probably will. It can't help itself.

"Well, you didn't tell Mom, did you?" asked Penny. The kind of trouble that Penny would be in if her mom learned she'd kinda sorta tampered with a famous painting wasn't something she liked to think about. Matthew didn't know about the letter's connection to the painting, but still. She couldn't take any chances.

"No," insisted Matthew, as the three of them headed down the long outdoor path from the ticket counter to the entrance of the museum.

"Is it, like, a secret school report?" asked Mason.

"It's—I want to surprise her with it," lied Penny. "Just this letter I found in a library book. My own little Paris project."

"Well," said Mason, "nobody at the Sport That Shall Not Be Named had heard of Marie Bonnet. But dude, that might not have even been her real name."

"What do you mean?" asked Penny. Obviously, *she* knew it was Marie's real name. But she wasn't about to let another brother in on her quest. Scorpions, the both of them.

"We're doing Euro history in my online class right now, and we were just learning that a bunch of girly-girl spies from Britain were in Paris during the occupation," Mason said. "So she might not have even been French. She could have been a secret agent. Like Nick Fury from the Avengers."

"It was her name," said Matthew. "We found her online. Pen emailed her daughter."

"*Cool*," said Mason as Penny reached over and slugged Matthew in the arm.

"You don't have to tell him everything," said Penny.

The museum *was* really interesting. There was

everything from small pins that members of the Resistance wore to a few copies of an old newspaper, *Défense de la France,* that they wrote to share news about the Allied movements and Resistance activity.

"Look," said Matthew, pulling her toward a giant wall near the front of the museum. "These are the names of known members. Maybe we can find Marie on here—or Héloise, or Adrien." The shiny wall had name after name written in gold metal, honoring the Parisians who had fought against the Nazis.

But as the three Markses stared at the wall, something quickly became clear to Penny.

"She's not here," she said. "Guys—there's *no* women at all!"

"There's not?" said Mason. "Huh. I didn't even notice." Penny narrowed her eyes. Of course he didn't. Mom would have. But the next words out of Mason's mouth made her feel a little better. "Dude, what the heck. That's so unfair."

"That's weird," admitted Matthew. "I mean, there were *tons* of women in the Resistance."

"There's hardly anything in this whole museum about the women. *Or* the kids," Penny pointed out.

"This thing talks about women," said Mason, pointing to a smaller plaque. Matthew hurried over and read it.

"It's talking about the female British secret agents,"

he explained. "Josephine Dalton, Sonya Butt, Virginia Hall . . ."

"But there's not much about the *Parisians*," said Penny.

"Sorry, Pen," said Matthew with a shrug. "Maybe Marie wasn't actually in the Resistance. All we know is that she wrote a letter. That's not much. Or maybe she *was* a member, but they just don't do that great of a job at honoring the women and the kids. Some things are just . . . lost to history. I saw on that display over there that only six women were given the award of Companions to the Liberation, even though *a thousand* men were, because they didn't really count civilian activity. It isn't fair—you're right. It isn't fair at all."

Delphine Ollier. Marie Bonnet. Jeanne, maybe, whoever she was. Women, creating beauty out of chaos, and being shoved out of history again and again and again. It infuriated Penny. It curled her stomach, right to her core.

Erin Drust had always been into manifesting. She learned it from her dad, she said—that if you thought positive thoughts, you could will things to yourself. A sunny day, or a million dollars, or an A on a test.

Well, Penny didn't believe in any of that, or she

would have willed herself home to Wisconsin back in September. She would have willed Mason home from the hospital that very first night, last spring.

Her mother always said the opposite—that when you stop thinking about something, it finally happens. "A watched pot doesn't boil," she'd say, reminding Penny that staring at her phone and waiting for Rosalie to text her back was a waste of time. If she occupied herself with some other activity, she'd probably hear from her.

She wasn't so sure that was true either. Why would forgetting about something make it happen?

So it must have been a coincidence that that night, as her mind was off of Marie Bonnet for a moment, something finally happened.

She started sketching.

Nothing crazy, just a macaron on a plate, with a piece of graphite pencil. But man—this felt good. Like going on a long bike ride on the first warm spring day of the year, when you realize you can wear sandals instead of boots. She remembered the feeling of creating something out of nothing. The way it stretched her wrist and relaxed her eyes. She hadn't sketched in ages. Maybe she would even paint it.

Maybe—

Ding. An email.

She glanced over. It couldn't be—it probably wasn't.

After all, it hadn't been yet, so why would it be now? That line of thinking made no sense, and she knew that, but whatever. Why get her hopes up? She sketched and sketched, ignoring the *ding* and filling out the thickness of the macaron, suddenly realizing she should have eaten more chicken at dinner because this thing was looking delicious.

It wasn't until she was crawling into bed that she thought to check her email one last time. And there it was.

Penny,
I apologize for the delay. This time of year is quite busy for me, as I'm sure it is for you as well!

My mother was, in fact, born in Paris. I did have an aunt Héloise, and she and my mother were very close. However, my mother moved back to France shortly after Héloise and my father died, within three months of each other. She currently resides in Paris, in an assisted living facility in the tenth arrondissement. Her name is Marie Jensen now.
I visit as often as I can; it was very hard on our family when she chose to move. I typically spend my summers in France so that I can be with her.

I've attached a link below if you'd like to contact the facility and reach out. I am very curious about the painting you found and would love to see a photograph of it if you've got one. Neither my mother nor Aunt Héloise ever spoke of their experiences in Paris during the war, but Maman loved art all her life.

Please do send that photo if you get a chance.
Warm wishes,
Odette

Matthew would have said boom shaka laka. Mason would have talked about some obscure soccer player named Odette he'd heard of once.

But it was Penny's email, and Penny's adventure. Yet she found, as she read the note over and over and over again, that there was something slowly sneaking its way up her throat: a desperation to share it. To tell someone, anyone, what she'd found.

February 1944

MARIE WAS DESPERATE to tell someone about the pieces of paper she'd left in the train station. Someone; anyone. Clarisse. Adrien. Héloise, who didn't want to hear it. Her sister went to work and came home, tight-lipped. Jeanne would come over and whisper with Marie at the table. Her sister still seemed furious.

Well, fine. Marie didn't care. That was Héloise: blustery, like Henri the baker's cat had been. You couldn't go right up to him and rub his belly or he'd claw your eyes out. No, you had to be cautious, letting him know you were there when he was ready. He would watch you from the corner of his eye, swishing his tail against the iron gate. Papa used to sneak him stale pieces of baguette. It took a year for him to even let Papa stroke him behind his ears.

But Marie had never felt like this before. Every

morning when she woke up, she was no longer a normal girl. She looked at herself in the mirror, and while her hair was still blond and her eyes were still blue, she felt her insides had completely changed, morphing into something unrecognizable.

She didn't just go to school, praise the marshal, wait in ration lines. She didn't simply wait for life to happen to her and dream of a day when she was older, when boys would wrap her fingers in theirs and whisk her to picnics on the Seine. Of a day when Papa would come back and tell her how proud he was of how she handled herself doing the war.

Non.

Marie was like Jeanne d'Arc. She was bold and daring and triumphant. She'd play her part to get les Boches out of Paris, and she knew Maman was smiling down on them.

Every day brought a new adventure, a new note slipped into her hand by Jeanne. She'd distributed papers, and sure, that was mostly her day-to-day task. But she was beginning to do more here and there. She'd stolen bicycles and torn down signs, under Jeanne's watchful eye. She'd distracted a German officer one day while Jeanne did something to his bag, and although she could barely breathe, she'd played her role, asking him about his family back home and tossing her hair like a silly little girl. She'd coughed too, startling him—Jeanne had taught her that the Germans were terrified of French germs.

One particularly cold February afternoon, Marie sat in front of the hearth, pretending it was blazing. She could almost make herself feel her fingers getting warmer, almost ignore the grumbling in her stomach. *Rations*—all well and good, until you showed up and there was no meat, even if you had your ration card. The Germans fed themselves first, always. Some days, though, she thought the soldiers looked just as hungry as she was. The thought of Adrien being able to sneak anything to her and Héloise was laughable. Her sister made boiled turnips almost every night. Even potatoes were rationed now. Potatoes!

There was a knock at the door, and Marie jumped about a foot. It wasn't the familiar knock of Adrien, and Héloise would of course have burst in. Soldiers, she thought, terrified. Her heart raced. They'd seen her tear down their propaganda; they'd seen her flash a *V* to Jeanne when she saw her on the street. They'd seen—

"Let me in, little rabbit," a voice sang out. Jeanne!

Marie exhaled slowly, trying to push all the nerves out with her breath. She felt her heart rate start to slow. Just Jeanne. As dangerous and daring as she was, Marie always felt like nothing bad could happen when Jeanne was there.

Marie unlocked the door and Jeanne barreled in, untwisting her long blue scarf from her neck. "This cold front will never end, will it?"

"There's frost on the inside of the windows," said Marie. "We can see our breath at night."

Jeanne smiled at her, eyes bright as ever. "We'll just have to make our own warmth then, won't we? Where's your sister?"

"The Ritz," Marie said, but she had no idea if that was true. Héloïse kept so many secrets from her, even now that they were on the same team. Marie did just as much to help Jeanne, didn't she? But still, Marie had caught her in lies. She'd say she was at work, but Marie would find her apron for the Ritz tossed across her bedpost. She'd say she was with Jeanne, but Jeanne would suddenly stop by to send Marie on another errand. Héloïse was not honest, not with her sister. Not anymore.

"I have something to discuss with you," said Jeanne. "Sit. I'll make us some coffee." Marie still hated the taste of coffee, even the bland ersatz kind that Héloïse made from acorns. But these days, heating her stomach was far prioritized over pleasing her tongue.

"There's so little coal, it will take ages for the water to boil," said Marie.

"Well, this might take a minute, so that's just fine," said Jeanne with a grin. She filled a small pot with water and set it on the stove before making herself comfortable at the Bonnets' tiny kitchen table.

"You still make things so lovely," said Jeanne, running her fingers across the white-and-yellow fringed table runner Marie had put out that morning.

Marie smiled. "That was Maman's. She found it at a charity shop, just before she died. She always believed in making our home as beautiful as possible, even though it was so small."

"Beauty," said Jeanne quietly. "What a concept, in a time like this, isn't it? To take the time to brighten the corners of our homes. It's an act of resistance all on its own, wouldn't you say?"

"Maybe," said Marie cautiously, sitting across from her friend. "But I'd also say there are far more important burdens to bear than an ugly kitchen."

Jeanne folded her hands and leaned forward, staring intently at Marie. "Would you?"

"Of course."

"Let me ask you this. What do you know about the Louvre?"

"The art museum? Maman used to take us there as

often as she could. It's empty now, isn't it? That's what the rumors are."

"Just about," admitted Jeanne. "Hitler fancies himself a great collector of art. But we French, we were smart. We knew when he came, he would raid our art museums and steal our most precious treasures. Most of the art that was in the Louvre was snuck out before the German boots even clomped across the Champs-Élysées."

"Where did it go?" asked Marie, fascinated.

"It was smuggled out. That's all we know." Hah. Marie doubted that. That was all *Marie* knew. But she always got the sense that Jeanne knew much more than she let on. It was as if she was allowing Marie to read a book slowly, page by page, holding the final chapters just out of reach.

"Plenty of other museums did the same thing, of course," said Jeanne. "But some did not, and the Nazis are snatching up every painting and piece of pottery they can find."

"But why?"

"To enjoy for themselves, of course. To hang on the walls of their gilded living rooms and glorious entryways." Jeanne's mouth twisted up as if she were to spit. "And also . . . well, Marie. I'm not sure I should tell you."

"Tell me," Marie insisted. "Haven't I proven that I can be trusted?"

Jeanne laughed. "That you have. Fine! Fine. Rumor has it that Hitler wants to create an art museum that puts the Louvre to shame. A museum that shows off the greatness of culture—the type of culture *he* approves of."

Marie shuddered. "I can't even imagine such a horrible place."

Jeanne sighed, tucking a chestnut curl behind her ear. "Neither can I, but I'm afraid many things are happening now that are beyond the imagination. And museums aren't the only things being plundered. Private art collections are going missing left and right. Family heirlooms."

"All for some fancy German museum?" asked Marie, confused.

Jeanne shook her head, her eyes staring intensely at Marie.

"It's about much more than a museum, little rabbit," she said. "It's about a people's culture. Art—we need it, as human beings. We need beauty just as badly as we need baguettes! It's not just about taking lives, you see? It's about taking what *matters* to people. It's about taking their very will to live."

Marie nodded. The small things she had of her mother . . . what if those were to be taken? Her teacup, with the gold flower pattern. The very table runner they had just been admiring. These were such precious things to her.

"Art stirs up our hearts," said Jeanne. "It reminds us of truth and goodness. And the Germans . . . that's the last thing they want. The French being reminded of who they *are*. Surely you've learned the Latin motto of Paris in school?"

"Fluctuat nec mergitur," Marie said. "'She is rocked by the waves, but does not sink.'"

Marie thought of the long afternoons she'd spent with Maman and Héloïse, wandering the never-ending corridors of the Louvre, staring at paintings that lit her heart aflame. The look on Maman's face—a dreamy look of hope, of admiration for the beauty of the French spirit.

"What do you need me to do?" Marie whispered.

"There are paintings we need to hide," said Jeanne, both quietly and quickly. "The last few bits of art les Boches haven't snatched up. From private collections of families who've been taken."

"Jewish families?"

"Mostly. They're being safeguarded by a very old man who lives in the sixteenth arrondissement. A couple of families who foresaw what was coming left their valuables with him for safekeeping, but nowhere in Paris is safe any longer. We need someone who can pass through crowds unnoticed. A schoolgirl, with a painting for her teacher in her knapsack."

Marie nodded slowly.

"I'm asking you to be very brave, Marie."

"I'm scared," she admitted quietly.

"Of course you are. You'd be a fool not to be scared. I wouldn't trust your judgment if you weren't scared. Scared is how you're feeling, but courage is what you're practicing."

"And where am I to take these paintings?"

Jeanne slid a piece of paper toward her. "Memorize this address, then shred the paper and bury it in a pile of snow. No leaving it in a satchel, like Héloise. Understood?"

Marie nodded again, and Jeanne leaned forward, tracing a cross on her forehead.

"Jeanne d'Arc will be praying for you," she murmured. "And so will I." For a moment—the first Marie had ever seen—Jeanne looked almost forlorn. Her cheerful spunk seemed to drain from her eyes, leaving an abyss of sadness.

"What's the matter?" Marie asked her.

"It's just . . ." Jeanne blinked for a minute, and smiled. A smile that didn't come anywhere close to reaching her eyes. "You looked so much like my sister, just now. I used to trace the cross on her forehead when she was feeling anxious too."

"You have a sister?" Marie asked.

With that, Jeanne snapped back to life. The mask she'd temporarily removed slammed down over her face, and her smile lit her features once more. "A sister? I apologize. I meant my niece. She's still a child, though, and you no longer are, in so many ways. I am sorry for that, Marie. I'm sorry for asking a thirteen-year-old girl who should be thinking about things like the cinema and boys instead of worrying about things much grander than her years."

"Jeanne d'Arc was only thirteen when she became a soldier," Marie reminded her.

"That she was," whispered Jeanne. "And you are every bit as brave as she was. One day, I will tell my niece all about Marie Bonnet, and how brave *she* was when called upon."

It was simple.

Marie Bonnet, who had once been just a normal girl, simply another face in a crowd of Parisians, would show up at the café across the street from where Adrien worked. She didn't look through the windows of Café Fleur-de-Lis anymore; he never had any food to sneak them, and even the black market had run dry on coal. Besides, she wanted to avoid calling attention to the fact that she was across the street so often. He'd wonder what she was doing there. And if she thought Héloise didn't approve of her activities—well. Adrien, the closest thing she had to a brother, would be horrified.

She'd go in, looking bored. Flop down at a table in the corner and pull out a book. She had to make sure that she actually read the thing, in case someone watched what page she was on or asked what it was about. She wanted to bring her book about Jeanne d'Arc, which she nearly had memorized, but Jeanne had suggested it might be a bad idea to read about a French hero in public. So instead she read *Treasure Island*, which sounded exciting but was actually incredibly boring. Buccaneers and buried gold? Who cared about such things?

Finally a huge woman with a mole on her chin would whip around the corner and start scrubbing the tables. When she got to the one next to Marie, she'd turn to her and snap, "Did your uncle make it on the train all right?"

Marie would respond with a simple "Oui, madam."

The woman would then reach into Marie's bag, take the rolled-up canvas, and lumber back behind the café counter.

And that was all Marie knew. Pick up painting from the house on tree-lined Avenue Victor-Hugo after school, bring it to the café. She'd done it three times now. Every time, her heart beat a little less quickly. Jeanne was right. Nobody was going to care about a thirteen-year-old girl with her nose in a book and her head in the clouds.

Life outside of Jeanne's errands had gotten so . . . *dull*. Clarisse's incessant chatter was obnoxious, and Marie's homework wasn't even graded. Most girls had to spend so much time waiting in the ration lines that they barely showed up to school anyway. And when they did, they had to grit their teeth and sing praise to the marshal. The marshal! Marie would spit in his face if she ever saw him. She would slap him so hard his cheek would remain red for a week.

But the sun was finally beginning to peek out from behind the clouds. April had blown away March with a great gust of wind. It was springtime, and the birds were finally returning to their nests in the chestnut trees along the Seine. Soon it would be summer, and perhaps by then the Allies would finally show up.

Marie hurried home from the café, feeling a small thrill like she always did. She stopped by Notre-Dame-de-Bonne-Nouvelle to light a candle for Papa, as Héloïse had requested, and tried not to think of wherever he was now. More and more boys and men were disappearing; Paris was nearly all women now. The ration lines were just lines of mothers, hungrily staring at the butcher and willing him to miraculously have meat.

Marie bounded up the stairs to her apartment but paused just outside the front door. She could hear a raised voice. Adrien?

"It's foolish, is what I'm saying," he said. "I can't believe—"

"Keep your voice down," another hissed. Héloise.

"What you're doing is dangerous," he said, his voice aflame.

"Of course it's dangerous! Living is dangerous. *Breathing* is dangerous. Adrien, look around. Being a person in Paris is dangerous, but we—"

"Think of what you're doing," he spat angrily. "To Marie."

Marie gasped, her hand to her mouth.

"I think of Marie every single minute of every single day," said her sister quietly. Marie had to force her ear to the door to listen. "I think of Marie every time I have to walk by a German, every time I remember where our father is, every time I have to hand another plate of food to a fat soldier speaking that disgusting language, talking about women, talking about Jews—"

"And what will happen to her, hmm? Are you thinking

of that? What will happen to her if you're shot in the street like a dog?"

Marie bit down on her finger hard to keep from crying out. How could he say such a thing?

"She'd be all right," her sister said evenly. "I know you'd take care of her."

A sigh. A pause.

"Of course I would," grumbled Adrien. "But you still should have told me."

"I'm telling you now. And anyway, I'm not sure how much longer—I'm not sure how much I trust . . . well. It isn't going to be this way forever."

"Let's pray so."

"And then . . ."

"Then what?" Now Adrien didn't sound angry. All of the fire had been melted from his voice. He sounded . . . different. Like his voice was topped with whipped cream.

Her sister laughed. *Laughed!* Marie hadn't heard Héloïse laugh in months. Probably even longer. Even when they were children, Maman and Papa had called Marie their sunshine and Héloïse their rain cloud.

Everything was quiet for a minute. Was everyone okay? Marie pushed open the door just a crack, and—

They—

They were embracing. Mouths meeting. *Kissing*.

Adrien was kissing Héloise, and not the sweet kiss on each cheek they'd learned as children to be polite and teased each other with endlessly. Not the fond smack of a kiss Adrien would plant on Marie's head on her birthday. No, this was the type of kiss Papa used to give Maman, the kind that entwined them completely and made the rest of the world dissolve into ash.

Quietly—as silently as she possibly could—Marie clicked the door shut.

Her sister and Adrien were—well, more than friends. That was obvious. For how long? Months, surely. That wasn't a *new* kiss, a trying-this-out kiss. Since Christmas? Since *before*? And Héloise had been keeping a secret from him all this time?

Héloise certainly had been keeping secrets. And not just from Adrien. This felt like the biggest secret of all, and she hadn't told Marie.

Marie flounced back out the front door, back into the sunshine.

Well, fine, then.

Marie could keep secrets too.

13

November, present day

PENNY WAS GETTING good at keeping secrets. When she told her dad she had to go do research for a history project, it was technically true, wasn't it? She didn't say *school* project. She just said project. And it was a project!

"I'm not sure if you should go off by yourself," Dad had said nervously. The bridge thing had shaken him, like it had everybody. He'd been spontaneously hugging her lately, which was more of a Mom thing. It was like he wanted to make sure they were all still there. He'd done the same thing after Mason had gotten so sick too. He'd once told Penny that every night in bed, he went through each family member in his head—Pippa's okay, Matthew's okay, Mason's okay, Penny's okay—and only then could he sleep.

"I'll be back in an hour. I swear," she promised. "I just want to go check out the American library."

"And you don't want to take one of your brothers?"

"No, Dad! I'll be fine." She did. She didn't. She couldn't decide. She wanted partners in this project, but she wanted the information to be all her own. She wanted company, and she wanted solitude. She wanted her brothers' help, but only on her own terms.

Mom saw the Delphine Ollier painting as her own personal project too. She'd been keeping Penny in the loop. They were trying to find the original owners, so that they could get the painting back to them, but that was proving hard to do. There wasn't much they *could* do. So much had been taken from so many people in the 1940s, and it was nearly impossible to track down whose was whose. But still—that was *somebody's* $5 million painting. It wasn't right to just hang it in a museum and pretend it was finders keepers. There had even been a law passed recently, Mom explained, that made it easier for public places like universities to return looted art to its owners without having to settle the ownership in court. France was trying to get things back where they belonged.

Marie Bonnet had to know something.

It wasn't hard to find the assisted living facility Marie lived in. Penny had never been to any kind of nursing home. Mom's parents lived all the way in Florida, and she only saw them once or twice a year. They were the kind of old people who still took river cruises and went salsa dancing. Both of Dad's parents had died before she was born. Rosalie's parents sometimes made her go visit her grandma in the nursing home where she lived. She mostly said it was super boring and smelled weird.

But the facility Odette had sent her the address of smelled fine—floral, almost, with a hint of Clorox. There was a woman with a tight blond bun and glasses sitting behind the front desk, flipping through a magazine.

"Bonjour," said Marie. Her mom kept reminding her that French people *really* appreciated if you started with a "bonjour"—you didn't just jump into your request.

"Bonjour," the woman responded kindly, glancing up at her. She said something in rapid-fire French.

"Um . . . désolée. Parlez-vous anglais?" "Sorry, do you speak English?" was Penny's most commonly uttered phrase.

"Yes," the woman said with a heavy French accent. "How can I help you?"

"I'm looking for someone," Penny said quickly. "Or . . . I'm here to visit someone." It occurred to her suddenly that they might not let her in if she wasn't a family member. She didn't have to lie, but she could at least sound confident. "Marie Jensen."

"Oui, Marie," the woman replied kindly. "She is expecting you?"

"Not—not exactly . . ."

"Then I must take your name." Crap—there was no way this woman would want to talk to a random stranger! Should she say she was a friend of Odette's? She should have had Odette give her mom a heads-up. Maybe she could call her or something. Should she—

A man suddenly barked something loudly in French, and the woman stood up abruptly.

"I am sorry. One moment, please," she said, hurrying out from behind the desk and racing down the hall.

Penny took a seat in the only chair in the foyer. She pulled out her phone and scrolled awhile, past photos of Rosalie and Erin at Culver's and in Global Leaders T-shirts and squeezing their cheeks together in Halloween costumes of their favorite singer—Rosalie was Daybreak-era Lucille, and Erin was fabulous Fairy-Tale-era Lucille. The world's biggest pop star had lent herself to a thousand different costumes this year. Matthew's former girlfriend, Courtney, was posting sad-looking selfies with long, rambling captions about finding herself. Hadn't *she* dumped *him*? Time to unfollow. Another student of Mrs. Marley's had gotten a scholarship to the Rhode Island School of Design—she'd posted a short video of herself opening up her acceptance letter and bursting into tears while some stupid song played in the background. Barf.

Then, this too: A girl from school, Harriet O'Something-or-other (O'Dell? O'Brien? O'Henry?), had posted an open letter to the Fernridge Falls school board, asking them to bring back the art curriculum.

Had Harriet been that into art? Penny couldn't remember. But, yeah, maybe—flashes of her chatting with Mrs. Marley about the best way to draw faces, her doodling in her math notebook when they were supposed to be solving for X.

"Art class is just as vital as math, science, or writing comprehension," the letter said. "We, the students of Fernridge Falls Middle School, deserve a well-rounded education."

Wait—now she remembered. Harriet was a transfer. She'd come from Lakeland Middle last fall, like so many other kids had after what had happened. It had been all over the news, just like Paris was now. That gun, and that boy—it had been terrible. Nobody had died but the shooter. But that didn't stop Rosalie from having nightmares about it. Rosalie had joined Global Leaders just afterward. "We have to do something," she'd kept insisting. As if they could do anything at all, really. They couldn't vote. They couldn't make a time machine and give the shooter a therapist or medicine or whatever he needed. Penny had worked on a painting about it, named *Peace*—it was a seashell in perfect condition, on a quiet, solitary beach. Caught in the tangles of driftwood. Rosalie had seen it and scrunched her face. "A painting?" she'd asked. "What's that go to do with . . . I mean, why?"

Because that was how Penny processed, that was why. Because that was how she made sense of things. Because she wasn't a letter writer, or a protest starter, or Greta freaking Thunberg, but an artist, that was *why*.

Why couldn't she have kept that feeling at Mrs. Marley's, when Mason was sick? Why couldn't she have remembered that then? Who was right—Penny or Rosalie? Jocelyn James or her very own mother? It all swirled around her until she felt dizzy.

Rosalie hadn't understood at all. She hadn't understood what Penny was trying to do or say. She had joined Global Leaders and started bringing Erin to their sleepovers. Then another town, another kid, another gun. The news vans left. That was that.

Penny snapped back to the waiting room and tried to ignore the obnoxious *tick-tick-tick* of the clock, but the woman didn't return. Five minutes, ten minutes, fifteen minutes. In fact, there didn't seem to be *anyone* around.

She got up and stretched her legs, glancing back to the woman's desk, and saw—

What was that?

A list.

A list of room numbers.

She shouldn't. Of course she shouldn't, but—

The painting. She *had* to know, and sometimes a person *has* to know things. It was strange, even to Penny, her need for that knowledge. She wasn't the kind of person who sneaked into Parisian nursing homes. She wasn't the kind of girl who sneaked a peek at room lists and ducked behind corners.

But she knew, looking at the painting, what Delphine Ollier was trying to say. About power in soft things, and about finding a window when you're in a dark, dark room. And she felt a responsibility to it like she'd never felt before.

Room 214. *Mme. Jensen, Marie.*

Penny walked as confidently as she could toward the elevator. She looked like she belonged, right? Just a thirteen-year-old girl, off to see her grandmother. Who would care? Who would notice? She hurried past a short row of glittering Christmas trees—wasn't it a little early for that?—and hit *up* as quickly as she could.

Penny couldn't help but glance inside a few of the rooms she passed by. People looked . . . *sad*. So unbelievably sad; the kind of sad that made Penny's heart leap into her throat. Most of them were watching TV or staring out the window. She hadn't even seen a single worker. Room after room of starched white sheets pulled tightly over beds, florescent lights, French news channels. Even though she'd just started her search, she couldn't wait to get out of there. Room 214 was at the end of a long hallway. It was open a couple of inches.

She knocked carefully. "Bonjour?" she asked softly, sticking her head inside.

A woman sat in a chair in the corner of the room. She wore faded, soft blue pants and a cream-colored sweater. And she looked—*old*. Old didn't even begin to describe it. This was, without a doubt, the oldest person Penny had ever seen in her entire life. Her face was stretched and tired, like a painting that had now been smudged. The woman simply looked at her.

"Bonjour," Penny said again. "Um . . . Marie? Marie Jensen? Marie *Bonnet*?"

This was ridiculous! How were they supposed to communicate? How was she supposed to explain—

"American," the woman said. One word, her voice flat. Penny startled a bit. "Excuse me?"

"American voice," the woman said. "Speak English.

Your French—it's not so good. I am Marie. Who are you?"

Of course—Marie spoke English! She'd lived in America. Duh, Penny. Although, seriously? She could tell from just her "bonjour" that her French sucked? She couldn't help it. Those long Wisconsin vowels didn't wear berets very well.

"My name is Penny Marks," she said quickly. "I'm . . . I'm American. Like you said. Your daughter, Odette, said you'd be here."

Marie wrinkled her eyebrows. "Odette . . ." Her voice trailed off, as if she was trying to place a name she'd forgotten a long time ago.

"Odette," Penny said slowly. "Your daughter?"

Marie closed her eyes. "Of course. Odette. Héloise suggested her name. And where is Héloise?"

What? How could she not know that her own sister had died? Well, Penny wasn't about to deliver *that* news.

"I need to ask you something, Marie," said Penny. She didn't know how long she had until she was busted. There was no way she was supposed to be in here. "Do you know anything about a missing oil portrait? A woman, painted by Delphine Ollier? It was found in an apartment in the second arrondissement. And there was a letter I think you wrote found along with it. I have a photo." She pulled out her phone and started to scroll, finally landing on the painting.

She held it out to Marie, who didn't take it. She just squinted, trying to see it clearly.

"And—and I have the letter here," said Penny, putting the phone down and pulling the delicate piece of paper out of her coat pocket. "Maybe if you just saw it." She handed the note to Marie, practically waving it in her face. The old woman finally reached out, her hand shaking slightly. Her eyes widened slightly, and a curtain of understanding fell over her face. Something in the words had clearly clicked open a corner of her brain that she'd left closed for a long, long time. She knew, now, that Héloïse was gone—Penny could tell.

It took so long that Penny was unsure Marie could even read the smudged handwriting. She turned to Penny slowly.

"Where did you get this?" she asked in a whisper. "I wrote this." Her voice was like a fragile sheet of ice, ready to crack at any moment. "When I was a little girl . . . this letter. That painting."

"In the wall," said Penny quickly. "In the wall, of this apartment on Rue de Augustine, and—"

"Rue de Augustine." She shut her eyes. "Oh . . . *oh*." She muttered something in French.

"Marie?" A sharp voice at the door. There was a woman dressed in white—a nurse, probably. She said something in French, and Marie waved a hand at her.

The woman turned to Penny, clearly confused. "Qui êtes-vous?"

"I'm . . . I'm a visitor. I know her daughter," said Penny quickly. Where was the friendly front-desk attendant when she needed her?

"Visiting hours are not until Saturday," the woman said sternly. "You must leave now."

Penny turned to Marie. "I'll come back. Is that all right? Can I come back on Saturday?"

She reached back for the letter, but Marie held it to her chest.

"Héloise," she said quietly. Her chin dropped to her chest, and her eyes closed. She started muttering in French. All Penny could catch was désolée—sorry—and another name. Adrien, maybe?

"Marie?" the nurse said gently. She turned and shouted to someone down the hall, who came hurrying in. Then she grabbed Penny by the shoulder and guided her back toward the elevator.

"You are Héloise?" she asked cautiously.

Penny's jaw fell open, just a bit, before she caught herself. "Héloise?"

"Héloise," the nurse confirmed. "She is always asking about Héloise, talking about Héloise, wondering where Héloise is . . . but we do not know who she is speaking of."

Penny shook her head. "No. I'm not Héloise."

She had siblings of her own. They were not this French woman. They had not seen the things Marie Bonnet had seen.

That night, Penny couldn't sleep. Of course she couldn't sleep. All she could see was Marie's face. All she could hear was that nurse asking if she was Héloise.

She lay in her bed and stared at the ceiling for what felt like hours but was probably only a few minutes. She got up and crept into the kitchen, searching for one of the cookies Mom had brought home from the bakery down the street.

"Ouch!" *Slam!* She had walked right into—

"Mom?" Penny winced, rubbing her forehead. "What are you doing awake?"

"What are *you* doing awake? I'm a grown-up."

"And it's normal for grown-ups to be wandering the kitchen at . . ." Penny glanced at the microwave clock. "Two a.m.?"

Mom sheepishly pulled a cookie out from behind her back. "When they're hungry and overworked, it is. Come get one. I'll make us some tea, and you tell me about the sketch you're working on. I saw the graphite smudges on your hands."

Penny grinned. *This*—this was what she'd missed

with her mom. A moment to hang out, just the two of them, without soccer stats and belch noises from her brothers. Back in Fernridge Falls, she and Mom had done teatime every Wednesday after school. All the boys had practice, and Mom would make an entire pot of Earl Grey, just for the two of them. Sometimes she'd even get scones from the bakery and light a fire in the living room fireplace.

She and Mom would sip tea out of the fancy china cups that Mom only took out for Penny, joking about how she couldn't trust the boys in the same room as something breakable, no matter how old they got. Penny could talk about her day and her friends and her homework, and somehow Mom was always able to make things seem a little brighter and a bit more bearable. They hadn't had teatime since Mom got the Paris gig.

They sat at the rickety table, and Penny took a long, hot sip.

"Shouldn't you be making me go back to bed?" asked Penny.

"The French are more relaxed with their parenting. I read it in a book. Now, spill—what are you working on?"

"Why do you care?" Penny griped.

"Because I love you, kid. And I love art. And most of all, I love *your* art. Now tell me."

"It's nothing important. It's just—a sketch . . . I can grab it."

"Go," said Mom, shooing her with her hand.

Penny obediently trotted off and returned with her macaron drawing. Mom held it up to the light approvingly.

"Fantastic, Pen. You haven't lost a beat. Look at that shading."

"Yeah, well. I've just been bored, I guess. But it's . . . it's just dumb." It was dumb, and Penny knew that now. Not nearly as important as whatever had happened at Rue de Augustine that upset Marie so much.

"What on earth are you talking about?" Mom asked. "Dumb?"

Obviously Penny wasn't about to tell Mom about the letter, or finding Marie. Mom would be furious that she'd taken something so old and potentially historically important. Penny was starting to worry it might even be illegal.

So, at first, she just said that the terrorist attack had made her a little nervous. That it made her look over her shoulder more often and made her feel unsafe.

But once she started talking, she couldn't stop. She talked about seeing the plaques on nearly every street in Paris, commemorating this member of the Resistance who was shot, or that one who was thrown in prison. She talked about the terrorist attacks that were happening *everywhere*, not just in Paris but in every single country in the entire world. She talked about Mason, and the night with the ambulance, and how now he had to wear his hearing aid and remember to keep its batteries fresh. She went on and on about despair, and destruction, and all the things people had lived through and seen and felt and—

"Penny," Mom interrupted gently. "I'm sorry. I shouldn't have let you see the news about that attack. I had no idea it would affect you so much."

Penny glared. "It's not just that. It's not like, 'Oh, sweet little Penny can't handle the big bad world.' It's that . . . I'm just sitting in my room, drawing a cookie!"

Mom cocked her head. "I'm not sure I'm understanding you. Can you say more?"

"It's like . . . think of church."

"Church."

"All of those—*statues*! And windows! The altar-cloth thingy with the gold around the edges! I mean . . . the *Louvre*, Mom."

"The Louvre," Mom said slowly. "The Louvre, and church, and your macaron sketch make you upset because . . ."

"Some paintings take, like, ages to make. People spend their whole lives working on them, sometimes.

Why would someone put so much effort into making something *pretty* when all of this stuff is going *on* in the world?" The beauty of Notre-Dame-de-Bonne-Nouvelle, or of Monet's water lilies—they almost suffocated her. How could she have just stared at those canvases and allowed herself to feel *hope*, when the world had such a mess around every corner?

Mom furrowed her brow in thought. "I don't think it's about making things *pretty*, Penny. It's about creating beauty and reminding people of what's good and true in the world. About making spaces that are the *opposite* of all of that hurt and destruction. People have created art in much worse times than this. People who were going through things we can't even imagine. Honestly, I'm a little surprised to hear this coming from an artist."

"Well, I'm not an artist," she muttered. Not anymore."

Mom raised an eyebrow. "Actually, that reminds me." She pulled out her phone, and with a few taps of her fingers, an email came up. She pushed it over to Penny.

"An email," Mom said. "From Mrs. Marley. Checking in. She asked if I'd show it to you."

Penny just stared at the phone.

"Well, go on," Mom said, chuckling. "Take it."

Penny slowly picked up her mother's cell phone. It

was the second email she'd received in a week that gave her butterflies.

Penny,
I've thought of you often these past few months. Last week, one of my students competed in the Madison Youth Art Show, just like you did last year. She got third with her portrait of her cat.

I hope that Paris is widening your horizons and that you find an adventure around every corner. Most importantly, I hope that you've found a way to create art, however that looks for you right now.
Your friend,
Mrs. Marley

Penny just glanced back at Mom. "A portrait of a cat?"

Mom put her hands up. "Hey, don't look at me. People and their cats . . ."

Penny almost let a smile fall across her face but fought it back.

"I'm sorry for how that happened, Pen," Mom said quietly. "How things ended with Mrs. Marley. I think you are too."

Mrs. Marley's face, as she ran out the door.

"I should go to bed," Penny said. "And so should you."

"I thought I was the parental unit," Mom pointed out.

"Yeah, but you've become one of those artsy Parisian moms. I could be up until four a.m. writing a sonnet, for all you know."

"Go to bed, daughter mine," Mom said. "And hey—remember what I said."

Penny nodded. "The thing about beauty?"

"No," Mom said, reaching over to squeeze her shoulder. "The thing about how much I love you, kid."

April 1944

PÈRE MAURICE SQUEEZED Marie's shoulder as she, Héloise, and Adrien left Mass. He told them to keep courage. Marie wanted to turn around and ask Père Maurice what *he* knew of courage, here in his safe church. What did he know of bravery, praying for freedom instead of acting for it? But Héloise thanked him and begged him to pray for Papa's return.

She was exhausted, as she was so often now; she'd delivered a painting Saturday and stolen a bicycle for Jeanne Sunday. Héloise had argued with her. While Héloise was at work, Marie was supposed to be standing in queue at the butcher. But it wasn't as if they were going to have meat anyway! Héloise reminded her that she had a duty to her family, to herself. But wasn't Marie's duty to France greater? Besides, Marie told herself at night, Héloise probably wasn't even at work. She was off kissing Adrien somewhere, leaving Marie home alone to wait in lines and freeze her toes off.

It infuriated her that her sister still hadn't told her about Adrien, and it infuriated her just as much that Adrien hadn't told her either. How could they team up like that? How could they *keep* this from her? Didn't they think she'd be happy for them?

And she was, mostly. Happy for them. There was no boy good enough for her sister, except perhaps Adrien, and no girl good enough for Adrien, except perhaps Héloise. But there was part of Marie that thought if Héloise had time for a boyfriend, *she* had time to go wait for the butcher, or do more to help Jeanne, who always seemed to have so much that needed doing.

Marie had beaten Clarisse to school that day, which was odd; Clarisse was usually one of the first pupils in the room. The bell rang, and Monsieur Bassot led them in the singing of praises to the great marshal. Still, Clarisse did not burst in, her eyes filled with laughter and her mouth waiting to whisper the latest gossip to Marie or anyone else who would listen.

She's sick, Marie told herself.

A stomachache.

Head lice.

But Marie had the knowing. The same knowing

she'd had about Papa not returning; the same knowing she'd had about Jeanne knowing more than she let on.

Something was not right. Clarisse was not sick.

Marie said nothing about it to Héloise that night when her sister asked about her day. But Clarisse wasn't at school the next day, either. Marie wanted to ask Monsieur Bassot, but something in her mind set off an alarm bell not to.

Instead, she formulated a plan in her head.

When the final bell rang and Monsieur Bassot's endless droning had finally, well, *ended*, she dawdled at the back of the room while Yvonne pestered him with questions about their upcoming arithmetic exam. Marie grabbed a few random books off the small shelf in the back of the room; nothing anyone would even notice was missing. She shoved them into her bookbag quickly, making sure nobody saw her.

She hurried to Clarisse's street, a leafy avenue only a few blocks from school. It was nice to see that the trees were finally returning to life, even if it felt as though the streets of Paris were not. But to Marie's surprise—and terror—there was someone standing outside the door of the Le Maire house. It was a tall blond man with a navy blue uniform, his trousers slightly too short. Her heart thudded down to her toes.

"Bonjour," Marie murmured.

The man simply raised an eyebrow at her. "Have you come to this house?"

Quick, little rabbit. It was as if she could hear Jeanne's voice in her ear. Act foolish. Act silly. A thirteen-year-old girl, tra-la-la, what did children know?

She giggled, hoping she sounded as stupid as she felt. "Monsieur Lavigne asked me to bring my friend Clarisse her schoolwork. She hasn't been at lessons in a few days, and it would be such a pity if she fell behind! Goodness, how tall are you?"

The soldier almost cracked a smile. "Twice of you, at least. You and Clarisse Le Maire—are you good friends?"

Marie wrinkled her nose. "Of course not. She never stops talking!"

The man chortled. Who *was* he? His French was perfect, nothing like the guttural, hoarse attempts of the Germans. "Well, you're right about that. But do you know her well?"

"Barely at all."

"Then why would your teacher ask *you* to deliver her books?"

"Because," Marie lied, puffing out her chest proudly, "I'm the best in the class. I'm spectacular at arithmetic, and Clarisse is *dreadful*. I know all of my times tables. Would you like to hear them? Seven times six is—"

"Quiet, girl," the soldier snapped. "For goodness' sake, you're just as chatty as the little brat. Girls don't need to know arithmetic, anyway. Unless it's to measure for the cooking, hmm?"

"Where *is* Clarisse?" Marie persisted, keeping a girlish tilt of stupidity to her voice. But her voice shook, just slightly. The fear that had been there had bloomed even brighter, a garden of flowers cascading down her throat to the pit of her stomach.

The man simply stared at her.

"Let me see those books," he said quietly, holding out his hand.

Marie handed over her bag, silently praying to Jeanne d'Arc that she didn't have any spare leaflets floating around the bottom of it. He dug through it, checking for pockets, and she yawned, opening her mouth as wide as it would go.

He glanced up at her, eyes narrowed. "These are just schoolbooks."

"I *told* you. Monsieur asked—"

"You can leave the books," he said. "Go home. And hurry up. I don't want to see you around this house again."

Marie dropped them and ran.

***

"Silly, stupid girl!" Jeanne was livid. Marie had never seen her like this. Her eyes were wide and angry, as if Marie had burned all of France to the ground. "Did you give him your name?"

Marie had run home as fast as she could, and the man hadn't followed her. She'd run past a church, slamming into an elderly priest. She'd run past the stalls at the flower market, once again bursting with springtime life. She'd run past the opera, with the phantom hiding inside. She'd run past the Ritz, wishing Héloïse could come and save her. She'd run all the way home, bounding up the stairs and slamming the door behind her, and she'd sat at the kitchen table, shaking. She was still there when Jeanne arrived a few minutes later with a pile of leaflets she wanted Marie to distribute.

Marie had told her the whole story, and Jeanne responded with what she'd feared: Doctor Le Maire had not been careful. The fault of his daughter, the one with the mouth. She'd told too many people of his spectacular feats; she'd trusted when she should've feared. He was gone, taken who knows where. Probably already dead. Clarisse and her mother were still in Paris, but they were on house arrest, guarded day and night.

"Of course not!" Marie hissed. "And I didn't say anything about—"

"You shouldn't have gone there in the first place. You could have asked *me*."

"How was I supposed to know you knew anything at all?" snapped Marie. "You tell me nothing! You ask me to run all over Paris—"

Jeanne stuck a finger in her face. "*I* ask? Or was it you who *begged*?"

Marie bit her tongue. Jeanne was right, of course. She *had* begged. Pleaded to help, and now here she was, bringing destruction to their door.

Clarisse. Clarisse, who drove her mad, to be sure, but still. Her friend. Unable to leave her house, living every waking moment terrified.

"Who was the man outside her door?" asked Marie nervously. "He wasn't a German."

"Of course not," snapped Jeanne. "He was French. Milice. Haven't you seen them walking around in that hideous blue uniform? They're Frenchmen who have completely betrayed their people. Like police, but much, much worse. Their job is to sniff out members of the Resistance, and I'm sure your little show on the Le Maire doorstep will have him here in no time."

Marie had never seen this side of Jeanne before. She'd been more tense than usual lately; quick to anger and short with her words. But this was downright explosive. It was nothing like the Jeanne who talked of her niece, or the Jeanne who called her brave.

Marie shuddered. "I gave him a fake teacher's name. I told him nothing about the school. And the book was an old one I'd snatched from the shelf. There's nothing for him to trace me. Paris is a large place."

Jeanne just looked at her. "It's large until it isn't. It was a careless mistake, Marie. You need a break. I've asked too much of you, and it's got you rattled."

Marie glared at her. "No, it hasn't! It—"

"Quiet." It was as if Jeanne had pulled a cloud over her face. She was no longer Marie's friend, or her more adventurous older sister. She was a military general, and Marie was simply a foot soldier who'd stepped out of line. "I'll come for you when I think you're ready. In the meantime, you stay out of trouble. And for heaven's sake, don't go back to your playmate's house. Héloïse was right. You weren't ready for this, and I shouldn't have asked you for help."

The word *playmate*—clearly meant to make Marie feel younger than she already did. But it was the words about her sister that sliced her heart the deepest. Jeanne left, shutting the door a little harder than usual behind her.

Marie went to her room and flung herself on the bed, her face burning with shame.

***

When Marie dreamed, she dreamed of bicycles.

Bicycles, rolling up and down the street, with nobody even riding them. Lines and lines of bicycles, and her trying to run along with them, trying to keep up.

"Stop!" she hears. "Stop—"

She turns and sees him: a man in a blue uniform, with hair as blond as the sun. She runs, runs as fast as she can, her skirt getting twisted around her legs.

"Marie, wake up," the man says. "Marie. Marie!"

Marie sat up, hard and fast. She was in her own bed in her own room, Héloise sitting next to her, clutching her hand.

"It was a nightmare," Héloise said soothingly. Marie was still angry with her sister for her secret, angry that she could smell a slight whiff of Adrien on her, if she wasn't imagining things. But she needed comfort, like when you're freezing cold and all you can think of is a warm blanket. So she fell into Héloise, pressing her face against her sister's chest and letting her stroke her hair.

"You're probably starving," Héloise said. "A nap in the afternoon—that's unlike you."

"I'm tired. I'm sorry."

"No need to apologize," her sister said quietly. "Jeanne let me know what happened. She can be so cruel, Marie. Pay her no mind. She doesn't understand that that was your friend. I . . . do you want to talk about it?" *Was.* Héloise was already talking about Clarisse in the past tense. As if she was like Sarah, never to be seen again.

Marie shook her head wordlessly.

"We should have left," said Héloise. "We should have left years ago. Papa should have sent us to be with cousins out in the country—"

"We don't *have* cousins out in the country."

"Somewhere else, then! We should have *left*, left like almost everyone we know. Papa kept saying it would be all right, that he would take care of us, that we couldn't abandon Paris, because that's where Maman was. He was a fool."

"Don't!" said Marie. Her face flushed angrily. How could her sister say such horrible things about their father? Their father, who was suffering horrors they probably couldn't even imagine?

"I will never forgive him," Héloise said flatly. "I will never forgive him, and I will never forgive myself. I'm sorry, Marie. If I had been braver, I would have taken you myself, and we would have fled."

Marie opened her mouth to push back, but Héloise simply held up a hand to silence her.

"I made you dinner," said Héloise, pulling her into the kitchen. "Come."

Marie followed her, still blinking sleep from her eyes. Dinner: an artichoke, boiled and mashed with the tiniest pat of butter placed upon it.

"Where is yours?" Marie asked.

"I ate while you rested," said Héloise. "I really am sorry, Marie. Shall I read a bit of *Jeanne d'Arc*?"

But Marie just shook her head. She didn't want anything that reminded her of Jeanne. She ate her artichoke quickly and told her sister she was going back to bed. It was already dark out, the streets bare and empty except for the forlorn *clop, clop, clop* of a German soldier patrolling.

She rolled back and forth in her bed, tossing and turning, unable to find a spot and unable to stop seeing the man in blue.

Had Clarisse seen her from the window? Did she know Marie had stopped by? What if the guard asked her who Marie was? What if Clarisse accidentally told him where Marie lived? Or told him where they went to school, and what their teacher's name was? What if they got to Jeanne and Héloise and Adrien through Marie? What if—

"Marie?" Héloise quietly whispered through the crack in the door. Marie clamped her eyes shut. She didn't want to talk about Clarisse, or Jeanne, or anything else. She just wanted to be alone.

Her sister tiptoed back into the kitchen, and Marie heard a soft clatter. Then, her sister crying. Slowly, Marie crept toward the bedroom door and looked out.

There was Héloise, her eyes on fire. She had Marie's dinner plate, and she was licking it clean. The few smears of artichoke Marie had left on the plate were gone. Her sister's face was ravenous and mad as she made sure every sliver of food was eaten from the plate. Her shoulders heaved as she gasped for air.

Marie put a hand to her mouth.

Outside, the wind blew so hard it knocked Maman's old flowerpot off the grate. It fell to the street, shattering into hundreds of pieces.

November, present day

A MUG OF hot chocolate slipped from Penny's hand and shattered in hundreds of pieces on the kitchen floor.

"Geez!" Mason jumped from where he was sitting on the living room couch, working through a history quiz. "Watch it, Pen."

"Thanks for the help," she said with an eye roll, pulling the broom from the tiny pantry. Everything in French kitchens felt tiny: the dishwashers, the microwaves, the stoves, the pantries.

It was Saturday. Penny kept glancing at the clock. Visiting hours at the elder care facility started early afternoon, and Odette had put her on the visitors' list. She tried to sit in her room and work on her macaron sketch to calm her nerves. She was almost ready to begin painting it. Maybe she'd do it in oils, like Delphine Ollier. She'd read the email from Mrs. Marley over and over again, letting the words sink into her. She'd even signed Harriet's save-the-art-curriculum petition, scrolling past the photos of Rosalie and Erin at the corn maze to find it again.

Because maybe Mom was right, she thought. Maybe art could be her own little way of making truth out of chaos. Maybe her *Peace* painting hadn't been a waste of time after all.

"Lady and gentlemen!" Dad called out, walking in the front door. Mom was just behind him. "Family meeting."

Penny slammed the sketchbook shut and went into the kitchen. Dad was sitting at the kitchen table, surrounded by her brothers and Mom. A platter of chocolate croissants was out, so Penny grabbed one. No matter how hard France tried, it couldn't get the Marks family to join its no-snacking habit.

"Everyone," Dad said, "we have some exciting news."

When you've already heard "exciting news," and it ended up being *terrible* news—terrible news that ripped you away from your best friend and took you across the planet; terrible news that made you feel like a stranger everywhere you went; terrible news that left you lonely and isolated and miserable; terrible news that had *ruined* your life—hearing it again wasn't exactly thrilling.

"Pippa?" Dad said.

Mom took a deep breath. "I think you all know how much I've been enjoying my work at the institute. And while it's been a lot of hours, it's also been very rewarding, and it feels like where I'm supposed to be at the moment. I've been doing a lot of teaching, not just research, and my students have all given me great reviews."

"Good job, Mom," Matthew said. Mom grinned at him.

"Thanks. It—yeah, it's just exhilarating. I had my quarterly review with my supervisor, and she let me know that . . . one of the full-time instructors has recently left her position in order to move closer to her family, out of the city. She—she asked if I would be willing to stay . . . longer."

There was silence at the table.

Penny's heart fell into her feet.

"Like . . ." Mason scratched his ear. "Like, how *much* longer?"

"Well," Mom said quietly, "it's not a temporary position. It would be for as long as I wanted."

"You mean forever," said Penny, her voice sounding hollow.

"This is an *incredible* opportunity," Dad stressed. "And things seem to be going pretty well for us here, right? I mean, there've been bumps in the road. Of course. But you're all doing so well in school, and you boys have gotten hooked up with your soccer teams, and Pen, Mom did all this research and found an art class you could take!" He said it as if he was handing Penny something on a silver platter, something that would make up for the dread she felt raining down around her.

"It's in English," Mom said, looking right at Penny, trying to make eye contact. She knew. She knew how Penny was taking this, and she knew it was not well. "A colleague told me all about it. Her daughter is your same age, and she's in it, and she's from Sydney. I thought maybe—"

"So we're staying," Penny said. "That's what you're saying. We're staying."

More silence. An agonizingly long silence.

"This is hard," Dad said. "Man, this—this is hard, right? But we're a family. We're a team, and we, the captains, have to make decisions that are best for the team. Right now, Mom and I think that staying longer in Paris is what's best for the team."

"What about—I mean, I just applied to UW. And Minnesota, and Northwestern . . ." Matthew's voice trailed off.

"All still options," Dad insisted. "We know that part of this decision will involve some hefty flight fees to go back and forth. We want to make that work. Or if you want my help looking at some online options, we can do that too. College is so much more flexible these days than it used to be."

"I'm down," said Mason. "Honestly, I like it here. But I kind of want to go to a normal school."

Dad nodded again. "Another conversation, but definitely something we can look into for next year."

"Congratulations, Mom," said Matthew. He still looked a little overwhelmed, but he was smiling. "I'm really happy for you."

Mason shrugged. "Henri was just telling me about an academy league he's in. Tryouts are in April." Henri was one of Mason's friends from his soccer league, who carried around a huge binder of soccer cards everywhere he went.

"Awesome!" said Dad encouragingly. He started talking about finding a larger apartment. Shipping over the rest of their stuff. How they would be going back for two weeks in June to see friends, and how they'd commit to going back to the US at least once a year. And how their cousins, Haddie and Natalie, could maybe come visit for their college's spring break. And who knew where time would take them? Who knew how long they'd be here? Who knew—

Who knew—

Who *knew*—

"Kid," Mom whispered, while Dad kept going. Penny looked up, and finally made eye contact with Mom. The two of them, always. In the sea of Marks boys, there were always the girls. Each other's North Star. Until one spiraled off into a black hole, like she was doing right now, leaving chaos in her midst.

"How could you *do* this to me?" Penny asked. She felt herself starting to panic, her eyes filling with tears.

Mom stared down at her lap. Dad stopped talking.

"Penny Lane," Dad stressed, "I know this is difficult. But this is a *very big opportunity*—"

"For Mom. For *one person*," said Penny. "We aren't a team. We're a dictatorship." Mom flinched.

"I'm sure it feels that way," she said softly. "That makes sense."

Way back in September, she should have reminded Mom that she *had* a job: taking care of Penny. How dare she want a new one? Had she hated being just a mom, all these years? Had she always been secretly wishing for an opportunity to shake their old life off like dust from her shoes?

"You owe me an apology," said Penny. "I—I *hate* you. You—"

"Penelope," Dad said evenly, "what would you like us to apologize for? I'm sorry that the world—and this family—do not revolve around you. I'm sorry that you have a roof over your head, food to eat, and a family that cares about you, even though you treat them with nothing but disrespect. I'm sorry that you have a mother who's worked incredibly hard her entire life to provide for you, who took a huge pause out of her career so that she could be at every class party and every field trip and every art show and every soccer game, who now has the opportunity of a lifetime. I'm sorry that *we* are being asked to sacrifice for *her*, for once in our lives. And I'm sorry you have such a terrible attitude about it and are so incredibly ungrateful."

Penny stared at him, blinking. Matthew and Mason sat in a shocked silence. Her dad had never—*ever*—spoken to her like that. Every inch of the happy-go-lucky nature he'd picked up in Paris was gone, sailing away down the Seine.

"Max," Mom said, "that's *enough*."

"Any of those apologies work?" Dad asked angrily.

She hated him. Hated him, hated Mom, hated her brothers, hated Paris, hated France, hated the world. She stood, walked to her bedroom door, and slammed it behind her as hard as she could. She slammed it so hard that a glass of water on her desk tipped over, spilling all over her sketchbook. Destroying her macaron drawing.

She sat in her room, her heart beating so quickly she

could feel it. The rage would eat her whole. It coursed through her veins, a plague unleashed. Nobody came to knock—not Mom, not one of her brothers, obviously not Dad. She heard them out there, going on and on. Plans. Plans for an unknown future. Everyone simply scooted over, covering the space she'd left.

She had to get out of the apartment. But she couldn't stand to walk past her family.

She went to the window and yanked it open. God, it was *freezing*. She grabbed her softest sweatshirt and pulled it on, not even caring that the giant Green Bay Packers helmet on the front made her look ridiculously American. But there was the fire escape she'd peered out at so many times. She hopped right onto it and hurried down, onto the Paris streets. She had no idea where she was going. But she knew it was as far from her family as she could get. This anger had sunk into her bones, and there it would stay.

It was bitterly cold outside, but the sun was shining. That helped, at the very least. It poked around a few streaks of violet-gray clouds while Penny shivered in her hoodie, annoyed at herself for forgetting her jacket.

Her dad's words echoed in her head as she walked. "Do not revolve around you." "Terrible attitude." "Incredibly ungrateful." The anger in his eyes—*her* dad. King of the can-do spirit and the fine-it's-fine; solver of problems and coordinator of schedules. Dad never got angry like that. Not even when he had to talk to big-time CEOs who were completely running their companies into the ground, or when one of the boys missed an easy goal. Not when he'd had to argue with the car insurance people after hitting a deer last year, or when the moving guys had dropped his favorite mug while packing up. *Never.*

Well, fine. He wanted a terrible attitude? He got one. And her brothers—neither of them had defended her. *Nobody* had said, "Huh, maybe it's a little hard to move across the world." Or "Hey, Mom and Dad, you lied." She had thought that they were finally starting to become a real team. She should've known better. The only person she could trust was herself. Penny would trade her family in a heartbeat, if she could. And she didn't care how terrible that made her sound. She felt the truth of it sitting on her shoulders, heavier than a thick overcoat. She hated them.

Okay, but this: She had a plan. She had somewhere to go. She had a *mission*, and apparently she was flying solo from here on out. She didn't want anything to do with her brothers, who had completely sided with her parents and didn't care at all how she felt.

Penny hurried down the winding streets, walking

so quickly she worried about tripping on the cobblestones. Even though it was so chilly, there were plenty of outdoor tables packed with tourists sipping coffee and nibbling from cheese plates. Cars whipped down the crowded roads as if they were on fire.

Marie's nursing home. There it was. All of her anger filled her, and she funneled it into courage, and she burst through the front door like a girl who knew exactly where she was going, even though she felt more lost than ever before.

"What I don't understand," Penny said quietly, "is how you got the painting in the first place. We're trying to figure out who it belonged to."

Odette had reminded Penny via email that Marie was old. *Old*, as in, forgets things a lot. *Old*, as in, her mind was slowly fading away like a painting exposed to the sun.

"Let me know what she has to say," Odette had written. "I've tried so often to hear about her childhood. If you can get her to share, please do."

"Jeanne," Marie said now. "Jeanne . . . she was always getting me into trouble. It was my fault, though. I asked."

"Was that your friend?" pressed Penny. "A girl from school? Was it her painting?"

"No. I never knew where they came from. I took them to the café, and that was that."

Penny started to get the same feeling she got when working on an art project that wasn't coming together just right—when the glowy possibility of the oils wasn't mixing quite right, or when everything looked flat and dull instead of sharp and lifelike.

There was a crash outside the window—two bicycles, slamming into each other. Someone yelling angrily in French, someone profusely trying to apologize in Irish-accented English.

"I stole bicycles," Marie said suddenly.

"You *what*?" said Penny. She'd seen that in the museum. That members of the Resistance had stolen bicycles. Did that mean—

"The Germans. They were everywhere. Every corner, every shop, every café. Adrien worked at Café Fleur-de-Lis. He was my neighbor. He and my sister . . ."

Marie turned and looked at Penny, their eyes locking.

"There's so much to say. But the letter," Marie said. "You wanted to know about the letter. The letter I wrote to Jeanne . . ."

Penny nodded.

"The *not knowing*," said Marie. "You almost can't

stand it. You feel as if your very soul will burst."

"Yes," Penny whispered.

"A secret that's pulling at the corners of your heart. Or an itch you can't quite get to."

"That's exactly it," said Penny. "That's just right."

"I'm good with words. My papa was a writer. And that *knowing*, that there is a secret, a secret you must uncover," whispered Marie, "is how I felt about Jeanne. She was angry with me, you see. But she could never stay angry for long."

April 1944

JEANNE'S ANGER DIDN'T stay long. She showed up only a week later, asking Marie to steal another bicycle and keep another secret.

The week before, bombs had fallen on Paris. The Allies, instead of showing up and actually being useful, were dropping fire down from the sky. There was a photo of the French citizens killed as they left the train station, and the Germans were hanging it from every surface they could find. *See?* The photos seemed to be saying. *See what those stupid Allies are up to? Do you see what they want to make of your beautiful Paris?*

"Les Boches think they can turn us against the Allies," Jeanne muttered to Marie as they hurried past a wall full of the photograph, printed over and over. "They don't understand that we know very well just why Paris is being bombed. It's *Germans* they're trying to hit."

But Marie did not understand. How could the Allies claim to want to help them, and then drop bombs on their people? How could more destruction possibly end the destruction taking place? She had already walked around in fear of Germans and milice—did she now have to walk around afraid of the *sky*?

She shoved the fear to the pit of her stomach. She imagined pouring acid over it and lighting it aflame.

Stealing bicycles was one of Marie's easiest tricks. Paris was filled with bicycles; their little cardboard license plates were easy enough to swap out. Marie felt bad, stealing them from innocent French people just trying to get to work or school. But the Resistance, Jeanne insisted, needed them more. They needed to get places quickly and to look as if they belonged. Marie remembered the streets being filled with cars when she was younger; now the only trucks rumbling down the street were those of the Germans.

Marie hadn't been sure if Jeanne would ever trust her again, but it was as if the opposite had happened. Jeanne seemed to favor Marie even more than Héloïse now. Héloïse still met with Jeanne, but the cautious optimism was gone from her eyes. Now it was suspicion. It was as if she no longer trusted their friend. Jeanne would start speaking in hushed tones at their small kitchen table, and Héloise's eyes would narrow, and the volume of her voice would lower. Héloise would deliver the information the Germans joked about at the Ritz, as she cleaned their toilets and scrubbed their floors, but Jeanne no longer stayed for a roll or a cup of ersatz coffee. Héloise asked more questions than necessary, and Jeanne would get frustrated and leave abruptly.

"You're listening to Adrien," Marie told Héloise one night. They laid with their toes pressed against the headboard of their bed, their heads where their feet should have gone.

Héloise simply glanced over at her. "About what?"

"About Jeanne."

Her sister pressed her lips together. "I'd trust Adrien with my life, Marie. He worries."

"He should worry about what will happen if the Germans stay forever," Marie said. "He should be doing more."

"Quiet," Héloise snapped. "Or did you forget who's been sneaking us food for the past four and a half years? Who's been helping us write letters, trying to find Papa? Who's been giving us any spare bit of coal he possibly can, even if it means going to bed colder than we are? Who's been letting me use his ration card to make sure *you* have food in your stomach?"

Marie glared at her. "You're just saying all of this because—"

"Because what? Because it's true! It's *Adrien* who's been helping us, not Jeanne."

"Because of . . . that! The way you say his name now. It's different."

Héloise simply shrugged, and a fire curled up in Marie's belly. Before she knew it, her mouth was open, and everything was tumbling out.

"I saw you," Marie said desperately. "I saw you, kissing Adrien in the kitchen. I saw you *ages* ago."

At that, Héloise's hand flew to her mouth, her blue eyes wide, and she just stared at her little sister. Well, *hah*. Marie had gotten her sister. Finally gotten her to shut up. Outside, the German boots continued to *click, click, click*. A thick, guttural voice talking to another, and loud, obnoxious laughter.

"You didn't tell me," Marie said quietly. "He's . . . he's like our brother."

Héloise bit her lip. "I'm sorry. I was going to tell you. I was. I just didn't—I didn't know . . . you've seemed angry at him, lately."

She *had* been angry at him lately. "He's rude to Jeanne," said Marie grumpily.

"Jeanne this, Jeanne that! We know nothing about her, Marie."

"You're the one who brought her into our lives," argued Marie.

"And sometimes I regret it," said Héloise. "She asks us to be in danger, constantly. You! You're a child. And for what?"

"To be *free*," Marie insisted. How could her sister not know this? Hadn't she been resisting the Nazis too? "To help France. That's more important than . . . than . . . than kissing goofy boys!"

Héloise threw her hands in the air. "This is exactly why I didn't tell you!"

Anger flooded through Marie's bones—hot, sharp anger. Héloise, always treating her like a child, like something to be cared for and coddled. That wasn't who she was anymore. That wasn't how any child in Paris was. Not now. Marie was brave, daring, courageous. Marie was like Jeanne d'Arc, saving France, and what were Héloise and Adrien doing? Daydreaming about their future? Ignoring the clicking boots outside?

"You kept a secret from me," said Marie, her voice thick with emotion. "You and Adrien both."

This wasn't the first time her sister had kept a secret from her, and it wouldn't be the last. But Marie was upset about more than that. It was that it could no longer be the three of them, now. It would always be Héloise and Adrien, and Marie on the sidelines. Her long childhood of chasing after Héloise and Adrien was only going to continue, and somehow would be even worse. Marie would always be on the outside of the two of them while they made decisions and whispered stories and became closer and closer, squeezing Marie out until she no longer existed.

"Maybe I did. And I'm sorry," said Héloise. "I really, really am. But Jeanne is keeping secrets from us now, Marie. I don't know what. And I don't know why. But I don't think she's who she says she is. I think—"

"Stop," said Marie, shaking her head and sitting up. "I'm not listening to you anymore. If you and Adrien are too frightened to help—" She regretted the words the moment they were out of her mouth.

"How dare you," seethed Héloise. "While you're off playing games, stealing bicycles, I'm eavesdropping at my *job*. What do you suppose happens if I get caught? Worse than being fired, I'll tell you that! Jail. *Worse.* And what happens to you? You're left here to starve!" Héloise picked up a pillow and threw it angrily at the window, making Marie jump. "You can say I kept something from you, you can say I'm being suspicious about Jeanne, you can even say I've been distracted by Adrien, because perhaps I have been. But don't you dare call me a coward, Marie Bonnet. Don't you *dare*."

Marie opened her mouth, ready to apologize. She knew Héloise was right. Her sister just made her so angry sometimes that words could flow out of her mouth like birds, quickly flying before she could stop them. But Héloise was up, storming away. She went into the kitchen and slammed the door, leaving Marie alone in the silent bedroom.

That night, as Marie lay in bed, she buried her face in her pillow and wished for Maman. The door creaked open, and she heard the gentle tiptoeing of Héloise. The bed dipped as her sister climbed in, and she heard the pages of a book turning.

"And when the British soldiers burned the cities," Héloise read quietly, "she did not hide in a field. She did not hide atop a mountain. She threw her shoulders back, triumphant. 'In God's name, let us go on bravely,' she said."

Marie kept her eyes closed, but pushed her feet against her sister's, their socks gently rubbing together for warmth. And she knew all had been forgiven.

The next day, Jeanne didn't show up at the apartment door, knocking and asking a task of Marie. There had been more whispers at school—*the Americans, the British, the Americans, the British*. Someone was coming to save them. Someone, and soon. They'd been saying this for years, but something was beginning to feel different. There was a crackle in the air; an extra burst of energy shooting out the seams. The soldiers seemed younger and angrier. Yvonne from school had been spat on for turning her back as a German soldier passed her on the street. Marie didn't dare go by Clarisse's home again, but she thought of her often, even willing herself to pray for her friend's safety to the God she wasn't sure was listening.

The sun was finally out too, ending days and days of gray. Marie would walk outside and, instead of shivering, turn her face to the sun. There were chairs outside the Café Fleur-de-Lis once more, the loud Germans taking up space on the sidewalk.

Marie burst into the apartment after school to find Adrien there, sitting at the table with Héloise. They both had serious looks on their faces, and she knew instantly that something terrible had happened.

"You aren't at work," Marie said, surprised. She could have been talking to her sister *or* Adrien; it was odd for either of them to be there right after school.

They glanced at each other.

"I've been let go," Adrien said quietly. "It's my birthday next week."

Marie furrowed her brow. "Why would that mean

you can't work at the café any longer? Monsieur Harold serves there, and he's ancient."

"You may have noticed that more and more men—and older boys, really—are gone," said Adrien. "That's because the marshal has ordered any man over the age of eighteen to go work in Germany."

She *had* noticed; of course she had. The streets of Paris were filled with women. The only men who seemed to be around anymore were les Boches. But Adrien didn't seem like a man to her. He still felt like a boy.

"You're leaving," Marie whispered. She could barely get the words out.

Adrien, gone. Adrien, the only brother she'd ever known, one of the only smiling faces she actually enjoyed seeing. He'd be sent away.

Off to Germany, like Papa, never to return.

What more could the Germans take from her? From her sister?

"Marie," said Héloise, taking a breath. It was only then that Marie realized they were holding hands over the table. "We're *all* leaving."

There was a beat of silence as the words worked their way into Marie's ears and cascaded down her bones.

"I don't understand."

"We can't stay in Paris," said Héloise. "Adrien will be

sent away. We can't keep living like this. We've barely enough food, and—"

"But the Americans—"

"We can hope and pray that they'll be here soon. But we can't wait around to find out," said Héloise. "And if they *do* come, it's sure to be bloody. A man Adrien works with at the café—he got us papers. We can leave, on the train. We're going to the countryside, to live with—"

"We can't," burst out Marie. "Héloise, how will Papa know where we are? And what of the rest of Paris? We'll simply abandon it to the Germans? Jeanne *needs* us. We'll just—"

"It's the only way!" Héloise burst out. She shot out of her seat, and Adrien winced at her anger. "It's our only choice. I've lost Maman. I've lost Papa. I am not losing Adrien, and I am not losing you. You've done enough, Marie. We've both done enough. Jeanne will be just fine without us. Your precious Jeanne! I'm your *sister*, and still you care for her more than me!"

"That's not true," said Marie sullenly. "I . . ."

"Marie," said Adrien quietly. He put an arm around Héloise, who leaned in to his shoulder. "Listen to me. Your sister's right. I understand that you want to help. That's a good desire. And you *did* help. You helped a great deal. But I am *not* going to Germany.

Me refusing to go is the biggest Resistance act of all, isn't it? Denying them a worker? The milice are everywhere, the Germans listen to everything—you're going to be caught, and sooner rather than later. Then I'll be in Germany, you'll be in jail, and what good will that do anyone? Listen. We'll go to the countryside, and stay with my friend's family. Just for a little while. The Americans will be here soon, and they'll liberate Paris. *Then*—no, just listen to me—*then* we return. Your father will return, and all will be how it was. We'll rebuild Paris. We'll find Jeanne. We . . . we'll be a family. All will be well. But in the meantime, this is what needs to be done."

Marie felt hopeless.

She couldn't rely on what Jeanne d'Arc would do, or what Maman would do, or Papa. Now she had to do what Marie Bonnet would do.

But then, another thought—

Héloïse, with the plate.

Héloïse, whispering secrets from the Ritz.

Héloïse, kissing Adrien in the kitchen.

Marie had promised her sister, hadn't she? Those few months ago, when she'd began working for Jeanne, she'd told Héloïse that her sister would never lose her, no matter what. Her sister had taken care of her this entire time, been both mother and father. If anyone in this brutal world deserved a happy ending, it was Héloise. Marie could be willing to burn at the stake, but she couldn't pull her sister up there as well.

Clarisse had thought herself invincible, and look at her now. Stuck in her house like a princess in a tower.

"All right," whispered Marie.

Héloise exhaled a sigh of relief, and the fire in her eyes slowly died out.

"We leave on Friday," said Adrien. "I'll come for you at half past five."

Marie nodded, her heart heavy with the weight of all she was agreeing to.

17

November, present day

PENNY SAT AND stared at her wall, heavy with the weight of all she'd learned the day before from Marie.

The nurse who'd come in to kick Penny out was the one who'd been at the front desk the first day Penny had attempted to visit. She was kind, but firm: Marie was elderly. She needed her rest.

Penny had been about to ask if she could come back tomorrow when Marie asked it of her instead. Penny got the feeling she'd been waiting to tell her story for a long, long time. She also had the feeling there was a lot of it left. After all, Marie said she'd been planning to leave Paris with Adrien and Héloise—but if that had gone according to plan, how had her letter to Jeanne wound up in the wall with the painting? And where had Adrien gone?

Now, it was just after Mass, and her parents had gone

to the bakery. Her brothers were home doing who knew what. Her mother was furious with her for not saying where she'd gone the day before, and her dad was still furious with her for her reaction to the Paris news, and she was furious with her mother for accepting a job that was ruining Penny's life, and she was furious with her dad for calling her selfish. All that fury: well. It was too much for a few eclairs to smooth over.

There was a knock at her door—the rough, fine-I'll-knock knock of a brother.

"What," she said flatly.

Matthew poked his head in. "You okay in here?"

"Why do you care?"

He exhaled, sharply, through his nose. "You know, Penny, I'm not the enemy here. I didn't decide to move here, I didn't decide to stay here, and I'm not thrilled about the plan either. So, if you want to be a brat about it, never mind."

Penny opened her mouth—closed it. Paused.

"I talked to Marie," she said.

Matthew shut the door, then thought better of it and called out to Mason.

"You should have brought us," whined Mason.

Penny had just shared all that she'd heard from Marie so far.

"She *was* in the Resistance! I knew it!" said Matthew. "Man, I would *love* to talk to her, Penny. Someone who lived through the occupation . . . I mean, *wow*." Matthew looked like she would have looked if she'd been offered a chance to sit down with Claude Monet.

"So where do you think Jeanne ended up?" asked Mason. "Like . . . one of those . . ." he looked sick to his stomach. "The camps?"

"It's hard to say. I couldn't find anything about *any* of them online, in terms of Resistance activity," said Matthew.

"I feel kind of dumb," Penny admitted. "I just . . . I didn't know that much of this."

"Don't beat yourself up," said Matthew, which was nice. "It's not your country. And besides, you think because there are all these World War II movies, people know about the Holocaust? They don't. Did you know they don't even *teach* the Holocaust at Fernridge Falls High anymore?"

"They think it's too gruesome?" asked Penny. "We read about it this year at the middle school." But, okay—Lila Porter *had* almost thrown up.

"No," said Matthew. "Because some people don't think it's real. Or they think the numbers were exaggerated. Jocelyn James had this whole spiel—"

Penny's jaw almost fell to the floor. She didn't want

to hear another word about that woman—that woman, who had soared into Fernridge Falls like a vulture and made it so horrible that Mom and Dad didn't even want to live there anymore. Not teach the Holocaust because maybe it wasn't *real*? Aliens, sure. Bigfoot. Unicorns. But the *Holocaust*? All these terrible things that the Nazis had done to Jewish people—to German and Hungarian and Polish and, yes, *French* Jewish people? And not just Jewish people, either. Romani people. Disabled people. Catholic priests. Anyone who fought back. So many sparks all snuffed out by such a terrible movement, and so much evidence, and Jocelyn James wanted them to—what, exactly? Shut their eyes?

She was about to tell her brothers to leave her room. To give her space. That this was her adventure, not theirs, when suddenly Mason said, "Hey! That's mine!"

Penny barely glanced over. She and her brothers were frequently stealing books from each other; he'd probably finally realized that she'd had his Captain Moonbeard comics since the move. But then she saw what he was looking at.

It was a painting she'd done last winter. It wasn't very good—in fact, it kind of embarrassed her. It was just a painting of a soccer player. Kylian Mbappé, from the French team. He was shooting a goal, and his eyes didn't look quite right, since she hadn't yet learned to keep the area around the tear duct a little lighter. The painting was propped up against her wall, along with the rest of her art that she couldn't bring herself to hang but hadn't wanted to leave back in Wisconsin either.

"No, it's not," she said. "I painted that."

"Yeah. Duh. But you gave it for me for Christmas last year, remember?"

"Oh." Wait, yeah—she had. Both of her brothers had gotten paintings of soccer players.

"I had it on the windowsill in my hospital room when I was sick," he said. That was right. Mom had taken it off his wall and brought it in for him. Later, after Mason returned home, Penny had seen it lying on a coffee table in their living room. She had taken it into her own room for safekeeping. In the Marks house, if something was just left out, one of her brothers would spill soda on it within minutes.

"You can have it back," Penny muttered. "It's not that good."

"Thanks," he said. "It . . . I mean, it's good to *me*. I looked at it all the time in the hospital. I thought about getting better and playing soccer again. It, like . . . helped."

"It did?" she said.

He nodded. "It reminded me."

"Of soccer?"

"Yeah. And of home." He cleared his throat. He didn't like talking about that time anymore than Penny did. "And just that—that there was this big old world out there to get back to."

Penny stared at him and Matthew.

"Come on," she said. "Get your coats."

April 1944

"DON'T FORGET YOUR coat."

"I won't."

"And a scarf. It's still chilly at night, and who knows how long we'll be gone."

"Héloise, I *won't*."

"And do you really need this old book? It takes up space, and we've read it so many times." The sisters were shoving things into one of Papa's old suitcases, preparing for their journey the following day. It was frayed at the corners, and heavier than their arms could manage for long. But it was also the only one they had, so they were hoping two dresses each would get them through for a while. Héloise had reached over and grabbed Marie's book about Jeanne d'Arc before Marie could stop her, and a small piece of paper fell from the pages.

"Paper? Where did you find spare paper? What is this?" asked Héloïse, grabbing it. Marie winced.

"I snatched it from school. Héloïse . . ." Her sister was reading the note she had scribbled on it, to Jeanne. Héloïse glanced back at her.

"I told you, Marie. We can't tell her we're leaving."

"But why?"

"Because," Héloïse told her, "she would ask you to stay, and I'm afraid you'd say yes."

"I told *you*. I'm coming with you." Marie had made up her mind. Of course she wanted to help Paris. Of course she wanted to help *Jeanne*. But she had made her sister a promise, one she was intending to keep. "It's just a note, for when she comes looking." Marie had written it just that morning. She couldn't bear to picture Jeanne knocking at the door to no answer, for days on end. She would leave the door unlocked and the paper on the dining table. Surely Jeanne was the only one who would come looking.

Wasn't she? After all, who would notice they were gone? Who would say, "Where has Marie Bonnet run off to?" Would Monsieur Bassot see that she wasn't at her desk any longer? Would Père Maurice wonder why they weren't at Mass? What about the woman at the café who always took her paintings? Would she wonder why Marie's courage had fled, or worry that she'd been captured?

The only person besides Jeanne who Marie really longed to tell was Clarisse. Poor Clarisse, who she'd spent all year being annoyed at. Locked up in her house like a prisoner. Was she wondering when Marie was coming to save her?

Even as she and Héloise shoved things into the suitcase and ate the last bit of mashed turnip they had, these were the things she thought about. She would become one of the missing ones, and it was highly unlikely that anybody was going to think twice of her disappearance.

A knock on the door—two short, one long.

"In the bedroom," Héloise called out. She was gently tucking Maman and Papa's wedding photo into one of her stockings.

Adrien walked through the kitchen and poked his head in. "Good. You're packing."

"Did you get the papers?" Héloise asked.

He nodded. "Did you tell the Ritz?"

"I'm not going to. I feel terrible leaving Madame Auzello in a bad spot like this, but I'm afraid if I tell her that we're leaving, she'll hold my last paycheck until she can find a replacement, which won't be easy. I need to go fetch it tomorrow morning."

"Good. We'll need every franc we can get," said Adrien.

Marie's heart lurched at the thought of leaving the only home she had ever known. But she had to admit one thing: the absolute safety she felt with Adrien and Héloïse. It was almost like having a mother and father. The sigh of relief she gave when she saw the two of them together—the feeling that for the first time in a long time, everything might be okay. Where they were did not matter. She had not belonged in Paris the last few years. But she belonged with Adrien and Héloïse, wherever they would lead her.

It wasn't going to be easy.

Adrien had train tickets, and the name of a man who was going to be wearing a red hat when he met them to take them over the mountains in Spain. It didn't feel like much of a plan, but it was all they had.

Héloïse was going to work for one last morning, to clean the toilets of Germans and collect her final paycheck. Adrien was off to pack his things and stay out of sight of soldiers. Marie was going to sit tight at home and wait for both of them.

Alone in their empty apartment, Marie shut her eyes. A thousand memories ran through her mind: Maman washing dishes at the sink, singing along to Charles Trenet on the record player that Papa had bought from one of his earliest book sales. Papa in his study, sketching yet another rabbit, trying to get the ears just right. Adrien, always Adrien, on the fringes of the room—sipping coffee with Papa in the corner, laughing with Héloise in the kitchen. And her sister, the person who would never leave her behind.

You can love a place as much as you can love a person, Marie realized. Paris was another member of her family. And it was her who was leaving it behind.

Someone knocked on the door, and Héloise froze. It wasn't Adrien's knock. Héloise obviously would have barged in. That meant it had to be—

"Open up, little rabbit," a voice sang out.

Jeanne!

Oh, no. Oh, *no*! How did she even know Marie was home? She hadn't seen her in over a week. Marie was equally thrilled to know that nothing had happened to her friend, and horrified that she was about to find out they were leaving. Maybe if she just sat extremely still, Jeanne would think she wasn't home?

Another knock.

But it was Jeanne. Marie had never been able to say no to her. Not since that very first day. For all her temper and all her secrets, Marie loved Jeanne like a sister. But now Jeanne was going to think that Marie had run off, scared. A little rabbit, indeed.

Marie got up and went to the door. "Come in," she said nervously. Jeanne gave her a look as if she was being strange—which she was—and followed her.

It only took her a moment to see the spotless kitchen, Papa's crucifix taken from the wall. The packed suitcase in the corner. The feeling of loss hanging in the air thick as a rain cloud.

She turned to Marie.

"So this is it, then," she said. Her tone was kind.

"I'm sorry," she said. "I would have told you, but I hadn't seen you in days. It was all so fast. Adrien—"

"The work order," she said. "He's not the only one. Most young men are leaving to avoid being sent to Germany. You'll need to be careful, little rabbit. They'll be watching. Especially for Adrien."

Marie's eyes welled up with tears. She'd been through so much, but this simple goodbye felt like it might be the final thing that put her over the edge. "I really am sorry."

"Don't be. It's the right choice." Jeanne ran her fingers along the edge of the table. "Actually, perhaps the apartment could be of use. Would you mind terribly if we popped in from time to time?"

"Of course not," said Marie. "Use it whenever you'd like." She had no idea how her sister would feel about that, but she didn't care. It was the least they could do.

"Now, a goodbye is in order," said Jeanne. "But that isn't why I came. I have one last thing for you to do."

Her heart sank. "I . . . I told Héloise and Adrien I'd wait right here. We're leaving as soon as—"

"It won't take but a few minutes, and Héloise's shift doesn't end for an hour yet," said Jeanne smoothly. How in the world did she know that? How did Jeanne *always* know these sorts of things? "We have one more painting."

A painting? Well, Marie could probably do that. She'd done this same errand plenty of times; surely she'd be back at the apartment before Héloise got home.

She glanced at Jeanne. "I need to do it right now, then." She'd been gripping the note for Jeanne, the one she'd planned to leave on the table. She slipped it into her pocket. No need for it now, and she didn't want Jeanne to know that she'd been planning to leave without so much as a goodbye.

"Thank you, Marie. I knew we could depend on you."

Marie should have known, as she looked back at that day. That fateful, terrible day, a day that haunted her nightmares for years and years. A day she'd do anything to forget. She should have known things would not be that simple.

Fetching the painting—that part *was* simple. It was

wrapped in canvas, like always; the man smelled of cigarettes, like always. The only difference was that it started to rain lightly as Marie hurried to the café. She tried to hold the painting under her coat to keep it safe. Well, better a bit wet than hanging in Hitler's museum, wasn't it?

Marie usually didn't open the paintings she took, but today she unrolled this one slightly, just before ducking into the café. She only wanted to make sure too much water hadn't splotched on it.

It was beautiful. It was colorful, and gentle, and soft, and bright. It was the kind of painting you wanted to stare at for hours. It was the kind of painting Maman would have loved. Marie had to admit that she was terrified—who knew where she and her sister and Adrien were going? Who knew when they'd return? Who knew *if* they'd return? But the woman in the painting didn't look scared at all. She looked confident. Her eyes seemed to say that everything would be all right. A flood of courage rained down on Marie, just as cold as the drops outside. The world was about so much more than this journey she was about to go on. There were such bigger things at play.

What was she doing? She needed to hurry. She rolled it back up.

Once inside, she noticed the café was almost empty.

There were two men sitting in the corner, talking over ersatz coffees. The woman behind the counter was scrubbing the nearly empty bakery case.

Marie flopped into her seat and waited for the woman to come over, like always. But she did not. In fact, she didn't even make eye contact with Marie.

Marie sat and glanced at her, willing her to come over, but still she didn't. Hurry up, madame! A woman came in and tried to order a croissant; the woman practically laughed in her face and told her she'd need to queue at the baker's for such a thing. She glanced at Marie, meeting her eyes for a brief moment, and still she didn't come.

Marie glanced at the clock. Héloise would be home any minute! Why wasn't the woman coming over to ask about her uncle?

Well, she had to hand off the painting. It wasn't as if she could take it with her to the mountains. She'd have to change the plan.

She walked up to the bakery case carefully.

"Bonjour," she said slowly.

The woman grunted and didn't look at her. "What do you want?"

What on earth? Why was this woman—the same woman she'd handed paintings to for months—acting as if she wasn't there? Why didn't she recognize her?

"Um . . . my uncle arrived all right," she said. "On the train."

The woman scowled at her. "What in the good lord's name are you talking about? Do you need to order something? If not, get out. I have customers to serve and no time to entertain little girls."

Marie furrowed her brow. "But—"

"I said go!"

Marie's heart sped up. What on earth was she supposed to do?

She turned to leave, and as she did, her eyes fell upon the men in the corner.

They were looking at her very, very intently.

Marie's blood turned to ice. She had to go.

She hurried out of the café as quickly as she could. Where to go, where to go? Should she simply leave the painting in her apartment? Yes, that would work; Jeanne could figure it out from there. Héloise was right about Jeanne—always getting them into sticky situations. Well, she could solve this one for herself. Marie was done. She was leaving Paris with her sister and Adrien, and that was that.

As she sped home, hoping to beat Héloise—oh, her sister would be furious!—she passed the corner of Rue de Augustine.

That was it! She could take the painting there. She

hadn't been to the house since the day she'd learned one of Héloise's secrets, but perhaps there would be some Resistance members there who could take the painting from her. Marie picked up her pace, hurrying past a man walking his dog and a small group of schoolchildren. She subtly looked around, making sure the men from the café hadn't followed her. Perhaps she was being paranoid. The woman at the café had simply been mistaken. Or perhaps she was tired of risking her life for France. Perhaps she, like Héloise, had fallen out of love with the Resistance and all it entailed.

Marie bounded up the stairs to the apartment and knocked quickly. Nobody answered. But what if . . . she tried the doorknob, and to her surprise, it was unlocked. But an even greater surprise was who was anxiously pacing in front of the window.

"Héloise!" said Marie.

Héloise ran to her and threw her arms around her. She was paler than Marie had ever seen her. "Marie! Oh, Marie—where *were* you? I got to the apartment and you weren't there! All I could think to do was find Jeanne! The *fright* you gave me!"

"She stopped by the apartment," Marie blurted out. "I'm sorry. I know you asked me to stay put, but she had one last painting she wanted me to get, and—"

"I'm just so glad you're all right. Oh my goodness. The things that ran through my head..." Héloise squeezed her eyes shut. "I completely panicked. I thought you'd been discovered, and arrested—I didn't know if the apartment was being *watched* or something."

"I didn't mean to scare you."

"Well, you did! I stopped by Adrien's quickly, to tell him I didn't know where you were. He went to see if you had stopped by Maman's grave. It was the only place I could think you might want to see before we left. I told him to meet me here. We need to leave the moment he arrives."

"Why is this door unlocked?"

Both of the sisters turned to see Jeanne bursting through the door. At the exact same time, all three exclaimed, "What are *you* doing here?"

"This door needs to stay locked at all times. Héloise, you know that," said Jeanne. "Although I suppose it doesn't matter, now that you're *leaving town*." Her voice was much sharper than it had been talking to Marie.

"What on earth were you thinking, sending my sister out on another task? You knew she'd say yes, even though I specifically told her to stay put," said Héloise angrily.

"It wasn't Jeanne's fault," Marie bit in. "*I'm* the one who agreed. But Jeanne, there was a problem. I went to the café, and the woman with the mole acted as if she didn't know me at all!"

Jeanne and Héloise both froze.

Outside their window, angry voices. "Where? Which one?"

"Was there anyone else in the café?" asked Jeanne, practically in a whisper.

"Um . . ." She thought as hard as she could. "Two men. Sitting in the corner. But they weren't Germans. They were French." Too late, Jeanne's warnings flashed through her mind. Milice. Frenchmen. Betrayers of their own people.

"What did you do?"

"I tried to tell her about my uncle, like always, and she told me to leave. And I did, but I didn't know what to do with the painting. I wanted to find you. So I came here," said Marie, confused.

The entire time Marie had known Jeanne, she had always been so calmly confident. She had an answer to every question, a solution to every problem. She made stealing bicycles and smuggling packages seem effortless. Even when she was angry, she remained in control, always knowing the next right move. She made the Resistance seem like a great chess game, one they were all playing together. One they could win.

It did not seem like a game now. The look on Jeanne's

face was one of sheer, ghostly terror. All the light and courage drained from her eyes.

"Oh, little rabbit," she whispered.

There was a sound on the stairwell. Loud, angry voices. Doors opening.

Héloise gasped, her eyes wild. Before Marie had time to think, Jeanne grabbed both of them by the shoulders and shoved them across the room. She pulled on the bookshelf, yanking it toward her to reveal a small door. Jeanne opened it and practically threw Marie and Héloise in before diving in herself, pulling a heavy strap on the back of the shelf so that it closed on them. The tiny room had yet *another* door, this one in the floor. She opened it and pushed the Bonnet sisters in. Marie coughed as she landed in a small crawl space, with barely enough room for three people to sit. Jeanne flopped down into Héloise's lap, then reached up and closed the door above them just as they heard the door to the apartment being flung open.

"Show yourself!" a man shouted.

Eyes wide with terror, Marie turned to look at Jeanne, who mouthed "Milice!" and held a finger to her lips. She grabbed the sisters' hands and squeezed them, as hard as she could.

"Out you come, little girl," said the policeman. "We know you came in here."

They heard the heavy boots pounding across the floor, opening cabinets and slamming them shut.

"She's not here," another voice said.

"Perhaps she somehow left without us seeing her," the first voice said again. "But look where she led us." Marie heard them moving papers. She'd brought these horrendous traitors to the belly of the beast. She'd shown them the Resistance's most important apartment in all of Paris! How could she have been so stupid? How—

"Héloise?"

Adrien.

Oh no.

No. No. No, no, no, no—

Marie turned to Héloise, eyes wide.

Chaos exploded in the apartment. Angry voices, telling Adrien to stop, to freeze. Adrien insisting he must be confused, must be lost, must be in the wrong place. Stomps on the floor, doors slamming, Adrien yelling—

Héloise tried to stand and leave, to save Adrien. Adrien, their dearest friend, who'd done nothing, who was only trying to help them. Tick, tock, Marie o'clock.

Jeanne grabbed Héloise, yanking her close. She threw her arms around her to hold her down. For a short woman, Jeanne had remarkable strength. Héloise opened her mouth to yell.

And in an instant, Marie heard the promise she'd made to her sister, those two months ago. That she'd never lose her.

What was going to happen, if Héloise dared to open her mouth? They would all be discovered. They would all be arrested. Perhaps they'd let Adrien go, but not likely. Marie and Héloise would be separated, thrown in cells in prison, or worse. They'd be shot. Shot like a dog, as Adrien had said. Héloise would lose Marie, just as she'd feared.

"You will never lose me. I promise."

Héloise had lost so much. Maman, Papa. School. Now Adrien. And now too, perhaps, Marie.

Marie threw her hands out to cover Héloise's mouth.

The look in Héloise's eyes pierced her heart. Like a window shade being pulled down. Héloise slowly realized what was happening, and what she would not be able to do.

Jeanne held Héloise to the ground, and Marie kept her hands over Héloise's mouth, even as her sister bit her.

"Quiet!" The *crack* of a gun hitting bone. A moan

from Adrien. Marie felt as if she was going to throw up. She squeezed her eyes shut and found herself begging Jeanne d'Arc to help them. Please, she shot up desperately. *Please—*

"We saw a little girl run in here," the policeman said. "A stupid little girl with blond hair. She had something very valuable. You are meeting her, yes?"

"I don't know any little girls," Adrien moaned. "I don't know what you're—"

Crack.

"We know that Café de Tulipe has been an outpost for Resistance activity. You've been caught. Your little scheme is up. Confess now, and we *may* be able to spare your life. Tell us where the girl is," the policeman said again.

A long, agonizing minute passed. Héloise tried her hardest to scream, but Marie and Jeanne held her as tightly as they could. Marie pressed her very body into her sister, muffling any sound she could make. She and Jeanne wrapped their arms around each other, silencing Héloise between them.

"It was me," Adrien bit out. "She had nothing to do with it. I've been paying her, and she's been helping me. But she is long gone. You'll never find her, and she knows nothing. I'm the one you want."

Héloise's eyes welled with tears, and they streamed

down her face. She shook with anger and sobs and determination to break out of her hold. When Marie looked at Jeanne, she saw that she was silently crying as well.

"Get him out of here," the first voice said. "Take him to Avenue Foch for more interrogation. I'm going back to the café to see if Aurelie recognizes him. If she doesn't, boy, you will be shot. So think long and hard about your answers to their questions. Meyer will have great fun with you. I'll lock up and send Alain to keep an eye out for anyone else coming or going."

"Hurry up. More could be coming any minute," the second voice said.

Adrien's moans of pain mixed with the soldiers' orders. They left, the door clicking shut behind them.

Marie stared at Jeanne in horror. She'd thought she was so courageous. She'd thought she could save all of Paris. But she had been wrong. She was just a little rabbit.

And what do little rabbits do?

They hide.

19

November, present day

HIDDEN IN A little corner of a very old nursing home, tucked away in the tenth arrondissement of Paris—known for its sweeping beauty and the bronze statue of Marianne, the French embodiment of liberty, equality, and fraternity—there was an old woman with a story to tell.

Penny sat in that room and listened. The three Marks children were silent, barely moving. Marie said "the Nazis" the way Penny might say "the annoying kids at school"; she said "Resistance" the way Penny might say "the neighbors." As if it were all commonplace; all simple. Penny heard about Jeanne and her fearless escapades, and about Marie snatching bicycles and distributing pamphlets. She heard about turnips and smuggled coal. She heard about a boy who was kissed in an apartment by a beautiful sister. She heard about a meeting place, a *secret* meeting place, where Germans did not go. And she heard about one last painting needing refuge, and one final meeting, and one boy taken away while three girls hid, silent as little rabbits.

The sun had gone down ages ago. They listened for hours, but finally, as Marie slowly trailed off and stared out the window, Penny noticed that she had a kink in her neck and both of her feet were asleep. She stood, shaking slightly.

"Did you ever hear from Jeanne again?" asked Penny. Her voice cut through the room, no matter how soft she tried to keep it.

Marie shook her head. "Non. I didn't need to. She was everywhere, after the war. A big hero. She wasn't even French—can you believe that? Héloise knew it, when we worked with her. She *knew* it, but never had enough proof. Her name wasn't Jeanne. It was Josephine, and she was from Kent."

"The SOE," said Mason. "The Special Operations Executive—the spies from England! I *told* you guys! Secret agents!"

Penny *shh*d him, but Marie smiled. "That's right. The British sent her and a lot of other women in to help the Resistance. She'd had a French aunt she was close with. She spoke the language, she knew the mannerisms. You can search for her, at the library. Or online—however you children search for things these days. She's in the museum. There's a plaque. . . ."

Penny nodded. She knew the plaque. The one Matthew had showed her.

"And she *did* have a little sister, named Mary," said Marie. "I learned about her long after the war. I think that's why she took to me. I suppose I should be grateful for Jeanne's service."

"Those agents from Britain were crazy brave," agreed Matthew.

"But it's an odd thing, to think you know someone, only to learn that you don't. Besides, everyone knows her name," said Marie, her voice turning slightly sorrowful. "And nobody ever speaks of Adrien. Nobody. He sacrificed himself for the Resistance in the end, and we didn't . . . we didn't even have a photo of him. There are so *many* people who should have plaques. Héloise and I never spoke of any of them. Nobody speaks about my sister, either, even though she spied on the Germans for well over a year and was the reason for plenty of valuable information being delivered to the Resistance effort. An entire train of German weapons was sabotaged because of information she smuggled. She was a hero, the little maid at the Ritz. But we went to America to forget. We never spoke of it, either—there's nobody to blame. Your family," she told Penny, meeting her eyes, "is all you have, in the end." Penny felt her heart lurch. *Her* family—well. She wasn't their favorite person at the moment.

"It's good you had each other," said Mason. He was curled up in the corner, in an uncomfortable-looking green armchair. "I wouldn't . . . I wouldn't want to be alone."

Penny felt something rise in her throat—tears, or bile, or guilt. "I always wanted a sister."

Marie smiled at her as if she was the only one in the room. "I always wanted a brother."

"Did your father—I mean, did you ever . . ." Matthew trailed off. Penny was glad he was there. Both of them. Obnoxious brothers, sweaty brothers. Her stupid big brothers who were her very own. Because she didn't want to be alone with this horrible story.

Marie shook her head. "He never returned, and we never received word. But that was how it was, after the war. So many people simply disappeared without a trace. It is likely that he died quickly once he arrived in Germany. Disease was rampant, and they worked even the strongest of men to death."

"What happened to Adrien? Did you ever learn?" Penny asked quietly. Is that what had happened to him too? Or had he been sent to one of the death camps, like Sarah? Or had he been killed on the spot? All of the possibilities seemed too awful to imagine.

Marie reached into her bedside table and pulled out a letter. Another insignificant scrap of paper that maybe wasn't so insignificant after all. She handed it to Penny, who opened it.

"It's—I'm sorry. My French . . ." Penny squinted.

Marie took the letter back, and read it in slow, steady English. Penny and her brothers listened, letting the words seep into their bones. They felt like they were in a dream. Not a tiny, cramped nursing home room. A dream, where three kids who weren't them were learning the fate of a man they'd never met, but somehow, felt like they knew.

This letter—this could change everything.

She glanced up at Marie.

"Why did you tell us all of this?" said Penny quietly. "You don't even know us." Marie's own daughter had said that her mother never spoke of her time in Paris.

Marie looked at her, and their eyes met. Suddenly Penny felt this: a spark, between them. A spark that could start a fire. And she knew, then, that it was true what Matthew had said. Everyone underestimated the women. Everyone underestimated the children.

"Because you look like I once did," said Marie. "What once burned in my eyes burns in yours too."

* * *

Penny and her brothers walked home in silence. Each of them was thinking, but not one of them shared their thoughts. They'd texted their parents that they'd be home soon, so that the whole of the French police force wasn't zipping around Paris looking for them.

When they got back to the apartment, Mom and Dad were sitting on the couch with wineglasses and serious eyes.

There were apologies first, of course. There had to be. "What were you thinking, running around Paris without permission again?" and "I have hurt feelings" and "I have hurt feelings too" and "I shouldn't have said that" and "I didn't mean that" and "I love you" and "I love you too." There was hugging (Dad) and crying (Mom) and awkward joke-making (Mason) and eye-rolling (Penny). It felt safe, in that little Paris rental. It felt like *belonging*. It felt a million miles away from Germans at the door and British spies.

It felt like maybe it was finally time.

So Penny pulled out the crumpled letter and handed it to her Mom.

"I thought—" Penny bit her lip. "I don't know what I thought."

Well, I'd thought I could solve the mystery of who the painting belonged to, and then we would get a huge reward and you could stop working and just go back to being my mom, but then I realized you had your dream job and never stopped being my mom, and I was being a selfish weasel just didn't seem right."

Mom's eyes widened as she read. "Pen—"

"Marie Bonnet was in the Resistance," Penny burst out.

"And Héloise was her sister," said Matthew.

"And Jeanne wasn't Jeanne at all!" said Mason. "She was Josephine Dalton, and she was British! I called that part!"

"And they were trying to escape because their friend—" started Penny.

"Their neighbor—"

"Héloise's *boyfriend*—"

Dad held up a hand, and they all fell silent.

"We need hot chocolate," said Dad. "Nobody say another word."

French hot chocolate was usually thick, like a candy bar. It was too rich for Penny. But Dad had Swiss Miss, sent in a care package from Aunt Juliet in Madison. And so, with hands wrapped around warm, steaming mugs, they told the story—again. The story they had just heard—from Marie's father being sent away, to her and Héloise escaping on a train. Soon enough—or much too late—their mugs were empty, and it was past midnight. "Your family's all you have," Marie had said, and Penny felt the truth of her words in that chilly Parisian living room.

"Wow," said Mom. She looked like she could cry. "Guys . . . *wow*."

"But wait," said Penny. "There's more."

"You sound like one of those infomercials," Mason joked. "Order now, and you'll get two extra sponges and a microfiber dish towel." But he too was leaning forward excitedly.

"She had another letter," continued Penny. "From Hugo Vannier. Adrien's great-grandson. He *lived*!"

"Hugo said that Adrien spent the rest of the war in a prison camp for members of the Resistance," Matthew said. "Not like concentration camps."

"Were they that different?" Mom asked. She rubbed her temple as if she was getting a headache.

"I mean—yes and no," said Matthew. "You had *extermination* camps, mostly for Jewish people. Think, like, Auschwitz. Then you had other, smaller camps for prisoners of war and people in the Resistance. The camps were still really bad, and tons of people died from starvation or disease. But they weren't sent there *to* be killed, if that makes sense."

"Not sure what the difference is if you wind up dead," muttered Mason, shivering.

"Well, Adrien made it through. Must have taken major guts, right? And after the war, he came back to Paris," Mason went on. "He lived there his whole life. Got married and everything."

"Hugo was going through some of Adrien's things after he passed away," Penny explained. "He was trying to learn about his family, during the war. And he found these letters—Adrien was looking for Héloise. He was writing to everyone they used to know, like old neighbors, and friends . . . but after the war, things were chaotic. So many people had just, like, disappeared. And then—well."

Penny was torn between feeling glad that Adrien had eventually moved on, met someone else, and had a beautiful life—a wife and kids and even a dog—and feeling sad that he'd never gotten to reconnect with his first love. It was like something out of a movie. Something out of a painting. Something that belonged in a museum.

"But then Hugo started trying too. We don't know how—but it worked. He didn't find Héloise. He found *Marie*," said Penny. "He wants to talk with her."

"That," said Dad, "is . . . *wow*." It was hard to shock Dad, but that was how he looked.

"She never even wrote back to him," said Penny. "She was too nervous. *Is* too nervous. She ran all over

Paris, fighting bad guys, but now she's too nervous to make a phone call."

Mom's hand was to her chest, and she just stared at the letter.

"Oh, Penny," she said. "It's hard, sometimes, to remember who you once were. It's the hardest thing there is."

They finally went to bed. They had to. There was still work, and homeschooling, even with this big, impossible story sitting on their hearts. Penny knew Matthew wasn't going to bed. He was watching YouTube documentaries, trying to find a mention of Josephine, the great secret agent, and her accomplices, sisters Héloise and Marie Bonnet. She could hear the soft buzz of ads for dog food coming under his bedroom door.

Just as she was about to finally fall asleep, Mom came in and sat carefully on the foot of her bed.

"Penny," she said. "I have to tell you one more thing."

Penny squeezed her eyes shut. Here it came—this was a historical document she'd stolen. This could impact decades of research on the Nazi occupation. This was—

"Being here has been really hard for you, and I see that," Mom said. "I want to do things to help. I really think we should enroll you with that art teacher I found, and maybe get you signed up for some actual classes. You can't spend all your time with your brothers, chasing down mysteries from the 1940s. I understand that."

Penny sat up and said the thing she needed to say. "It feels like you're so busy all the time now. Like all those years of being just my mom weren't . . . good enough, and now you have to do something else."

Mom grabbed Penny's face with her hands and turned it so she was looking right at her. Eye to eye.

"Penelope Rose," she said, "being your mom is the greatest gift I have ever been given. It is my first and favorite thing. I am doing something else now too. Something I've wanted to do for a long time, and now the time is here, and it's in Paris. But that doesn't make me any less your mom."

"It made me feel like you didn't like how things used to be," said Penny.

"I liked how things used to be, *and* I feel like it's time for a new season," admitted Mom. "I loved your field trips. I loved your class parties. I was the greatest classroom mom Fernridge Falls Elementary had ever seen, remember?"

"You did make one heck of a Valentine's Day card box."

"I'm an artist, haven't you heard?"

Penny bit her lip. "We don't belong there anymore, do we?"

Mom pulled her closer, and Penny leaned in to her shoulder. Mom smelled the way she always did: like oil pastels and slightly burned coffee. No matter where they lived, that Mom smell would stay the same.

"We belong where we are," she said. "And right now, we're here."

It started to rain outside, a gentle pitter-patter that seemed perfectly Parisian. Her mom yanked her into a hug, and there, she let herself be held.

April 1944

JEANNE YANKED THEM out of the compartment.

"We only have a minute," she said. "They're coming right back." Marie was silent, her eyes wide as dinner plates, and Héloise was gasping for air. Jeanne grabbed their elbows and practically threw them to the back of the apartment, tugging open a window and jumping out over the fire escape. Marie and her sister followed quickly, wordlessly. When they got to the bottom, the three of them tore down the street until they got to Notre-Dame-de-Bonne-Nouvelle. The rain had finally stopped, but puddles gathered on the street, reflecting the shimmer of the sun as it began to peer out. Jeanne pulled them inside the church and let the heavy door slam shut before glancing around to make sure it was empty.

Héloise reached out and slapped her. *Hard.* Jeanne's

head flew back, and the noise echoed throughout the cathedral. Marie put a hand to her mouth.

"You," seethed Héloise, "*you—*"

"You never should have told him about the apartment!" said Jeanne angrily. "You've endangered hundreds of people, you stupid, stupid girl!"

"Hey!" shouted Marie, rage curling up her belly. "Don't speak to her like that!"

Jeanne and Héloise both hushed her, their *shh*s seeming even louder than Marie's anger.

"You've killed him," said Héloise, in a quiet, dead tone.

Marie's jaw dropped. No. No, surely they were taking him to jail, and when they learned he knew nothing, he'd be freed. He was just lying to get out of the house, to get the soldiers away from them. He would escape. He would meet them. They would leave, the three of them.

"You have done that yourself," said Jeanne flatly. Héloise slapped her again, on the other cheek. Jeanne, to her credit, simply received it.

"Stop," said Marie, her eyes filling with tears. She reached for her sister's hand, and Héloise snapped back as if she'd touched a snake.

"Don't touch me," she said to Marie, her voice sounding hollow. The flickering candles illuminated her face and the giant painting of Jesus on the cross behind her. His eyes held a sorrow that rivaled Héloise's. "I can't . . . you . . ."

"I had to," Marie said desperately. "What would have happened if we had screamed for him? We would *all* have been arrested, and we would have been separated, and—"

Héloise stuck her finger in Jeanne's face. Jeanne rubbed the side of her cheek, wincing in pain. "You tricked my sister. You put her in danger. And I know you're not who you say you are. I *knew* you were a liar. But now I know you're a murderer too. You let an innocent man be taken for absolutely nothing. Nobody knows what they're doing to him, or where he'll be sent, or if I'll ever see him again. I will never, ever forgive you for this."

"You will never see me again, either," said Jeanne quietly. "You must forget we ever knew each other. You owe that to the Resistance."

"I owe the Resistance *nothing*, but I will forget your hideous face with pleasure," spat Héloise.

Jeanne turned to Marie, who stood shocked.

"I need to go," she said softly. "I want you to forget me, but I will never forget you, little rabbit."

Héloise stood in front of Marie. "Don't you talk to my sister. Leave us."

Jeanne and Marie held eye contact for just a moment,

and Marie realized with a start that the painting—the very thing all of this had been for—was still in the compartment of the apartment.

"Goodbye," said Jeanne. She turned, and was gone.

There was a step behind them, and the Bonnet sisters both jumped with fright. Héloise, who seemed as if she wanted to throw Marie into a pit of fire, still grabbed her and held her tightly. But it was only old Père Maurice, his hands in the air.

"I can help," he said quietly. "I'm here to help."

Adrien and his false papers were gone, but Père Maurice knew someone who knew someone who knew someone. The father of the parish, it turned out, knew many, many people. Perhaps as many as Jeanne. For once in their lives, they were in the right place at the right time.

The sisters slept in the church for the night, shivering under old altar cloths, while misty stars twinkled through clouds of froth outside. In the morning, the priest gave them papers and a blessing. A gruff-looking man with a giant mustache showed up and walked them to the train station. Once inside and barreling toward who knew where—the man wouldn't even say—Marie turned to Héloise.

Her sister hadn't cried. Not a tear since slapping Jeanne. She also hadn't looked at Marie.

"Héloise," she said. "I'm sorry."

Her sister closed her eyes.

"I'm sorry," repeated Marie, her voice cracking. "I shouldn't have left the apartment. I shouldn't have trusted Jeanne. It's all my fault." Jeanne—her note to her. She put her hand in her pocket. It was empty. The note must have fallen out during their scuffle in the secret compartment. What if a Nazi found it and connected it to her? Connected it to the painting? The pit in her stomach that had been sitting there since Adrien had been taken grew another eight sizes. But what were they to do now? They were on a train, heading far away.

"It is Jeanne's fault," said Héloise flatly, opening her eyes. As if she was speaking to a stranger. It's Hitler's fault, was what Marie was truly thinking, but she couldn't make her mouth form those words. This was not a time for logic, or for arguing.

"I shouldn't have stopped you from shouting out, and I shouldn't have put us in danger, and I shouldn't—"

Héloise put her head on her little sister's shoulder. She put an arm around Marie and hugged her close, tightly.

"I will try to forgive you," she said softly. "It's the best I can do."

The scenery outside flew past them.

"Where are we going?" Marie asked tentatively.

"I don't know," said Héloise. "But wherever it is, Marie, we will be together. We are little rabbits no more."

Marie wanted to turn and look behind, to where they had been. But she didn't. She leaned back in her seat, pressed her eyes closed. Said a prayer for Adrien. Another for Papa. For Clarisse, for Sarah, for all of the disappeared ones. Focused not on where they'd come from but where, full speed ahead, they were going.

December, present day

THE UBER DROVE full speed ahead, whipping around the Place de la Concorde. Penny stared out the window, taking in the magnitude of where they'd been and where they were going. It all felt big, now, and connected, as Penny would go around Paris—*there*, that's the hotel where Héloise worked. *There*, that's the house where the Resistance would meet. *There*, that's the church where Père Maurice spent Sundays preaching and Mondays organizing fake papers for Parisians to escape the city. *There*, and *there*, little spots of courage, little embers of a fire. She stopped at every plaque, now. She stopped and pressed her hand against it and thought, for a few moments, of the person who'd died there.

"You know," said Mom. "It looked pretty good." She was holding out her phone, showing Penny the picture she'd snapped. There it was, on the wall of the Musée de l'Ordre de la Libération. The letter, behind a thick layer of glass, with a small temporary sign saying that it had been written from Marie Bonnet, a member of the Resistance, to SOE agent Josephine Dalton.

A lot of things changed, after that. A lot, and not so much.

There was the letter, now in a museum for anyone to see. A letter that pinned Héloïse and Marie Bonnet into the archives of time, and recognized them for what they were: kids, girls, heroes. A letter that named Adrien Vannier as a hero too. This letter was no small thing; Marie was already getting requests from reporters to interview her. A man writing a book about children's involvement in the Resistance wanted to have her on his podcast. Penny had to explain to her what a podcast was. A radio show, on the internet.

There's this too: the painting, *A Mother at the Window* by Delphine Ollier. It was still being studied at the art institute where Mom worked. Penny visited it sometimes, admiring its coloring, feeling as if Delphine was there with her. They would try to find its owner. Marie didn't know who to ask, but now that they knew which agent the Bonnet sisters worked with, they might be able to get more information about Josephine Dalton's contacts. There was a family out there who it belonged to. They would find them, somehow, even if it took years.

There's this: Dad, on the faded couch. They needed new furniture, but Parisian delivery people weren't American. They told you a month out that they might show up, and you just crossed your fingers and waited.

"I'm sorry," he said. "I'm sorry I exploded at you about staying here, Penny Lane. I really am. I wanted you to love it in Paris, so badly."

"You didn't care that I was sad. You didn't care that I was struggling." She started to cry a little bit. She almost stopped and apologized, but she didn't. Her dad should see this: her very realest self.

He nodded. "I know. I did care, but I didn't show it. Maybe I didn't care *enough*. I wanted us all to just be happy for Mom. She's given so much to all of us. But you, Pen—you've given a lot too, haven't you? You're such a good kid. I'm so glad you're *my* kid."

Maybe that's what Penny needed to hear, most of all.

"You never *say* I've given a lot," she said. "It's always just—everything's great! Isn't everything amazing? Isn't this awesome news? It wasn't great, or amazing, or awesome. Not to me."

"Oh, Penny Lane. I should have acknowledged that earlier. It's good for Mom, and hard for you. I think it *can* be good for you too, or we wouldn't be here. But right now, it's hard for you. I can say that, if that's what you need. I think sometimes," Dad said, "I feel like I need to make the world seem as bright as possible. Because—because I brought you here, kind of. I want to make sure you know its potential. I want you to see how beautiful it can be."

That, she could understand. So she hugged Dad, and he hugged her, and the delivery people from the furniture store showed up that very afternoon with a new green couch.

And this: a girl, in Paris. A family that was shifting, changing, growing into something new. The stupid soccer games she had to go to—*football*, now. The long afternoons of reading books and drinking tea. The art teacher Mom had found her, who had bright red hair and an Australian twang to her English. She didn't say that Penny had promise. But she did say her shading was good, and Penny would take that. A couple of girls and their moms who she and *her* mom got together with once a month; expats, groaning about how much they missed Target but admitting that the desserts in Paris were so much better. Penny couldn't paint the peace that she was finding. But that didn't mean she wasn't trying.

Lastly, this: an old woman, older than any that

Penny Marks had ever known. Thinking, Why did I tell those children those things, when I haven't even told my own daughter? Thinking, Why would anyone make this much of a fuss about things long past?

But knowing the answers. Because our stories, well—they're what we have, when everything else is gone. When our people and places have been taken from us, we have our stories, and those who are willing to listen to them.

She would tell Odette. She would tell her granddaughters. She would make sure the secret of Rue de Augustine didn't die with her. Everyone knew about the great Josephine Dalton, but soon everyone would know about the great Héloise Bonnet. It was easier, perhaps, to tell stories to people you didn't know, and to have unfamiliar faces hearing them. But perhaps that was the flicker that would begin it all.

Seeing that painting again—that she now knew had been painted by someone named Delphine Ollier. A mother, by a window. It had given her courage, back in 1944. It gave her courage now. If things like that could exist in the world, well, it wasn't all bad, was it? The things we walked through. The things we survived. They were parts of the story, yes, but there were other parts. Courage. Laughter. Mothers by windows.

She held a pencil in her shaking hand. Her eyes were watering, but she blinked back the tears. There was still so much beauty to behold.

Dear Hugo, Marie wrote.

She had a story to tell about his great-grandfather, if he had the courage to hear it. A spark, not yet snuffed out, but rising—not hot like a blaze, but warm like home.

AUTHOR'S NOTE

Although I've lived in Wisconsin all my life, Paris has always held a special place in my heart. My great-great-great-great-great-great-grandparents came to Canada from France, and Paris is one of my favorite cities to visit. Croissants, the rolling Seine, the Shakespeare and Company bookstore—what's not to love?

But the city has a heavy history, and the story of the German occupation can be felt on many streets. You can scarcely walk a block without finding a plaque discussing something that took place during those difficult years. In 2021, I was sitting in the Ritz hotel with a friend, and I could really feel all of the history that had taken place there—the secrets, the stories, the scandals.

And there, Marie's story began to bloom.

Marie, Héloise, Adrien, and Jeanne are not real people—but they're inspired by real members of the Resistance who fought to free Paris from the Nazis. When the Germans invaded Paris in 1940, some French people took advantage of the new power structure, and some French people rose up to try and fight against the Nazi soldiers in large or small ways. Most Parisians fell somewhere in the middle: attempting to survive, which meant going about their everyday lives surrounded by Germans while finding ways to keep their patriotic spirit alive. Resistance was a dangerous job with deadly consequences. And out of the tens of thousands of French involved in the Resistance effort, 2,000 of those brave patriots were under the age of eighteen.

Why were children so important to the Resistance? Just as Jeanne tells Marie and Héloise, soldiers did not often expect children to be participating in political activity—they seemed harmless. Many of these children were as young as eleven or twelve years old, and the youngest acknowledged by France was only six. His name was Marcel Pinte, and he would smuggle information under his shirt. Due to a program called the service du travail obligatoire, or STO, a lot of men like Papa were sent out of France to work in German factories under horrible conditions. That left women and children to do a huge amount of Resistance work. But while their efforts were hugely important to the effort, they've often been overlooked. Their civilian Resistance activity, like smuggling or distributing information, wasn't seen to be as valuable as sabotage operations. Of the 1,038 people who were awarded the Compagnon de la Libération—a medal that thanked them for their service to their country during the occupation—only ten percent of them were under age twenty; and only 0.6 percent of them were women.

The Hôtel Ritz, where Héloise worked, was, and is, a very real hotel in the heart of Paris. The hotel was taken over by German soldiers and forced to hang a Nazi flag while its staff catered to the luxurious whims of the German elite. That made it the perfect place for the Resistance to have eyes on, in order to track German activity. The hotel's manager and his Jewish-American wife, Claude and Blanche Auzello, were involved in the Resistance, and the Jewish hotel bartender Frank Meier was so effective in smuggling information and passing along fake identification cards that the Nazis classified him as a "fanatic enemy of Germany." It's easy to imagine a young maid like Héloise picking up on all kinds of valuable information as soldiers chatted over breakfast.

What about Jeanne? Josephine Dalton, who the Bonnet sisters knew as Jeanne, is based on the many real-life women who were sent into France by the Allied nations to help set up Resistance networks. Women like Virginia Hall, Odette Sansom, Noor

Inayat Khan, and Nancy Wake worked as spies in France. They pretended to be French—even to most of the people they were working with. They were women who often grew up understanding the French language and customs, but they also went to special training schools that taught them everything from how the French held silverware to what kinds of clothing French people wore.

These spies had incredibly difficult jobs: not only did they have to recruit courageous Parisians to their mission, but they had to organize complex networks of information and make sure everyone was trustworthy, even under immense pressure. Many of them, unlike Jeanne, were eventually captured and sent to concentration camps.

While Marie was devastated by the loss of the Jewish community in Paris, many of the French disagreed. Between 1942 and 1944, tens of thousands of Jewish people—including children, like Marie's dear friend Sarah—were arrested and sent to death camps. In July 1942, French police forced 13,000 men, women, and children to stay in the Vélodrome d'Hiver under horrendous conditions for five days before being transported to their death. The French government didn't formally acknowledge their role or apologize for the roundup of Jewish people until 1995.

Jewish people weren't just killed en masse throughout Paris—they were also stolen from. While Marie's clandestine smuggling of paintings was a figment of my imagination, it very well could have happened. The Louvre, one of the world's most famous art museums, smuggled out a great deal of its famous artwork in 1939, and many private art collectors entrusted friends with their art if they left the country or believed they would soon be arrested. Hitler really did have dreams of a giant art museum and stole many valuable pieces of art from museums and private citizens, especially Jewish people.

The effort to hide artwork from the Nazis was gargantuan. It wasn't just about money—works of art are often priceless family heirlooms that help people remember who they are and what they believe in. Around 60,000 works of art found in Germany after the war were eventually returned to France. France is still in the process of returning these treasures as it slowly identifies theft victims. In 2019, the country formed a task force in order to locate Jewish owners of Nazi-looted artwork, and in 2023, French parliament unanimously passed a law that will help facilitate the return of stolen artwork to families by laying out basic guidelines instead of having to deal with every case in court.

World War II was one of the worst time periods our world has ever experienced. My own husband's family was personally touched by the war—one of his great-grandfathers spent much of the war in a Nazi Prisoner of War camp, and his other great-grandfather was active with the Polish Resistance. If we don't tell these stories, and remember these heroes, what will be left of them? According to the Anti-Defamation League, antisemitic incidents have spiked across the globe in the past few years. The George Santayana quote "Those who cannot remember the past are condemned to repeat it" quickly comes to mind.

Lastly, schools across the nation continue to slash their funding for art departments, insisting that an education in the arts takes away from "core classes." Mrs. Marley and I might ask: core for who? The core of what? Only sixty-nine percent of middle school students have art education integrated into their school days. It is a scandal of the highest order. Even for those among us who draw stick figures well into our thirties, an arts education (including music and theater) can help promote problem-solving, empathy, and creativity—all traits that are at the core of what it means to be human.

The problems that Marie and Penny were facing may look different today, or in your area, but they're still there, simmering just under the surface. I hope this book helps you think about how you can make a difference in your own community, and use your voice to defend truth, goodness, and beauty—however that looks for you.

ACKNOWLEDGMENTS

Not many people can say that they're doing the thing they've wanted to do since they were in kindergarten. I can. And I wouldn't be able to without my very own A-team, Alyssa Miele and Alex Slater. The two of you have shepherded my career in ways I never could have dreamed of, and I will forever be grateful that you took a chance on me.

The entire team at HarperCollins is top-notch, including Rosemary Bronson, Laaren Brown, Erin DeSalvatore, and many others whose touch made this book what it is.

The first time I went to France, I was accompanied by fellow travelers on the Catholic Feminist Pilgrimage. I think of you all so often, and I was flooded with memories during the writing of this book. You've been a gift to me.

I often quip that I would never be able to function without my army of babysitters. This book in particular would not exist without Brooke Tlachac, Maria

Courchane, and Julia Landowski caring for my little ones so well.

Any mistakes you find in this book are my own, but I'm indebted to so many other authors whose research helped me immensely, especially Ronald Rosbottom, Lynn H. Nicholas, Tilar J. Mazzeo, Sonia Purnell, Larry Loftis, and Alex Kershaw. I'm also thankful to the Musée de la Résistance Nationale and the Musée de la Liberation de Paris, both of which house collections that added so much texture and detail to the experiences of the Bonnet sisters.

Thank you to Sophie Barocas for the absolutely gorgeous cover—it's one of my favorites, and I'm tremendously grateful we were able to work with a Parisian artist!

I have so much appreciation for the readers, librarians, and bookstore owners who have supported my work for years, with a special shout-out to the team at Pauline Haass Public Library in Sussex, Wisconsin, as well as Lisa Baudoin and her team at Books & Company in Oconomowoc, Wisconsin.

Thank you to my entire family for their endless support: my parents, Mark and Grace Courchane, my many siblings (the OGs and the outlaws), and my plethora of nieces and nephews (Nora, Otis, Josie, Colette, Thomas, Sam, Leah, and Liam), who bring me so much joy. The iPhone note that holds my family's quotes and quips just continues to grow.

To my three wonders, Benjamin, Teresa, and Bridget: Thanks for your patience. I'm sorry for all the times Mom has had to google *just one more thing*.

As always, gratitude to Krzysztof, who has expanded my worldview in ways I never thought possible. I'm glad this story we're living is ours.

Most importantly, thank you to the Creator, who gave us the beauty we cherish and always points us toward truth and goodness.

Lastly, Marie's story is fictional, but there were many brave children who really did resist tyranny, and I'll never be able to fully grasp their fortitude. Not enough of them are publicly honored. I hope this book paid the tiniest testament to their spirit and memory.

May children across the globe know lives of peace.